A GEORGIANA

LITTLE BURIED SECRETS

CHERYL BRADSHAW

NEW YORK TIMES BESTSELLING AUTHOR

At what point then is the approach of danger to be expected? I answer, if it ever reaches us, it must spring up amongst us.

—Abraham Lincoln

1

Margot Remington exited the wood-lined boardwalk at Moonstone Beach and pedaled her bike onto the highway. It was dusk, and the sky had started to grumble, the clouds shifting and bending as they turned a melancholy charcoal color. Rain was coming. Margot could smell it in the air. But after the fight she'd just had with her older sister, she wasn't ready to return home yet.

The argument had started out as a simple one, with Margot asking Bronte if she could borrow a blue sweater.

"Why can't you wear you own clothes?" Bronte had asked.

"I want to wear something I haven't worn before," Margot said. "I can't afford to buy new clothes until I get paid on Friday."

"Why is it so important? Where are you going?"

"I'm meeting Sebastian later tonight."

"I thought the two of you broke up."

"We did," Margot said.

"There's no reason for you to see him. He cheated. End of story."

"I never let him explain his side of things. I feel like I owe it to him to hear what he has to say."

"I don't believe you. I think you're looking for a reason to get back together with him. If you take Sebastian back after what he did, you're an idiot."

The argument had escalated from there until Bronte got so heated she'd slammed her fist onto the kitchen countertop. Desperate to get away from Bronte's over-the-top drama, Margot had hopped on her bike. She needed time to think, to process all the cruel things her sister had said.

Margot and Sebastian had started dating a year earlier, even though she'd had a crush on him for the last three years. In her sophomore year of high school her body had started to change. She grew a couple of inches and developed curves in all the right places. Sebastian swooped in, and the two began dating.

For years, Margot had dreamed about dating Sebastian, and when the dream became a reality, it was just like she thought it would be. She was happy … until one night when Sebastian's parents had gone out of town, and he decided to throw a party.

The get-together was supposed to have been an intimate one at first—a few close friends, nothing more. Once word spread, it wasn't long before the party turned into something else:

Alcohol.

Dancing.

Loud music.

Partygoers stripped down to their undies doing backflips into the pool.

The drinks were flowing, and Margot knew it wouldn't be long before even more shenanigans began. As she scanned the drunken crowd, Sebastian had come up behind her, wrapping his arms around her waist. She'd found it cute at first, until his hands wandered, and Margot suggested they take a break from the party. She grabbed Sebastian's hand and helped him to his bedroom, relieved when he fell asleep a few minutes later.

With Sebastian out of commission, Margot took over the party, keeping a close eye on everyone and everything. She played the perfect hostess, picking up after her fellow classmates, refilling snacks, and trying her best to keep everyone in line. As the party wound down, Margot helped people find a safe ride home, and then she went to check on Sebastian. When she entered his room, she slapped a hand to her mouth, shocked to find Sebastian butt naked next to Kaia Benson, the new girl in town.

Sebastian insisted nothing happened between them.

Margot left Sebastian's house in a fury that night, refusing to speak to either of them until a couple of days ago when she ran into Kaia in the girls' bathroom. Kaia apologized about what happened at the party, and then she said something interesting—after giving it a lot of thought, she wasn't sure what, if anything had happened with Sebastian. Every time she'd thought back to that night, it was all a bit of a blur. Blurred lines or no, even if Kaia *was* telling the truth, Margot couldn't help but wonder what would have happened if she hadn't walked in when she had.

After her conversation with Kaia, Margot found herself trying to find a loophole—any loophole to justify giving Sebastian another chance. He'd gone above and beyond to win her back, and before the incident, he'd always been a stand-up guy, someone she could rely on.

Yesterday evening, Margot texted Sebastian. He'd replied right away, and they decided to meet tonight for dinner. Glancing at the time on her watch, she realized she'd have little time to freshen up if she didn't return home soon. She began pedaling faster, slowing when a car driving in the opposite direction swerved, its headlights blinding her as it bounded her way. Margot slowed to a stop, realizing her mistake when the car showed no signs of reducing speed.

In a split-second, Margot had collided with the car, and she found herself hurtling through the air, her bike going one way as she went the other. So many things went through her mind in that moment as she thought about her life and how much she didn't want to die.

There would be no meetup with Sebastian.

Not tonight, or any other night.

2

The following morning

I woke feeling off, and I wasn't sure why. Glancing at the clock on my nightstand, I realized I'd risen later than normal, which wasn't like me. Most days, my body was its own internal clock, and I never had to set an alarm. So why was today different than all the rest?

I had one sneaking suspicion.

Several months ago, I'd started feeling hotter than usual, and given it was December, I should have been reaching for my coat. Instead, I'd been stripping it off, fanning my face with my hand. I'd also felt tired and rundown, and I'd been forgetting things, like where I'd placed items in the house. On top of it all was a change in my mood, which was requiring a lot more effort to keep balanced.

At a recent Sunday dinner at my mother's house, she caught me fanning myself and suggested I get some bloodwork done. I put it off for a couple of weeks, but she kept pestering me until I relented. I made an appointment with Dr. Rae Remington, a woman who was also a good friend. As it turned out, my testosterone levels had just about flatlined, and there was a simple explanation why: I was entering menopause.

Yippee for me.

Upon hearing the news, my first question was how long the menopause madness would last.

It was a good question, but it had a less than satisfactory answer.

Seven to fourteen years on average.

Fourteen flipping years of menopause?

I couldn't bear the thought of it.

Even now.

I slid out of bed, rolled out my yoga mat, and did a quick fifteen-minute morning meditation session. Then I got in the shower. When I finished and stepped out, I realized I was no longer alone in the bathroom. Luka, my Samoyed, was sitting on the floor. He was staring up at me, his head cocked to the side like he couldn't understand why he hadn't been served breakfast yet.

"I know, boy," I said. "It's coming. Let me get dressed, and you'll get your breakfast."

Once he heard me utter the word *breakfast*, he spun around in gleeful anticipation. I reached down, smiling as I gave him a pat. I put on a pair of gray, high-waisted trousers and a violet, short-sleeved wrap blouse, and we hit the kitchen.

Dog food for him.

Eggs for me.

Eggs for him.

And it was time to go.

I grabbed my coat, even though I doubted I'd need it, and walked to the car, opening the passenger-side door. Luka hopped inside, and we headed to the office for a morning meeting with fellow private investigators Simone Bonet and Lilia Hunter.

Business at the Case Closed Detective Agency had been slow of late. For me, anyway. There had been no murders to investigate, no major crimes committed around town. I supposed it was a good thing, but it had left me feeling antsy and in need of a stimulating case.

I turned onto the highway leading into town, reducing my speed when I spotted Rex Foley's car parked on the side of the road. He was the chief of police for San Luis Obispo County in California. He was also dating my sister, Phoebe. I considered driving by and not stopping, until I noticed Foley was standing next to Detective Amos Whitlock, their eyes fixated on what appeared to be a mangled bicycle.

I pulled behind Foley's car and parked, which shifted his attention. He looked over and shook his head at me, like he wasn't surprised I'd turned up. I told Luka I'd just be a minute, and then I got out of the car.

Whitlock, who was dressed in a navy turtleneck, matching trousers, and a pair of shiny black shoes, grinned at me and said, "Lovely to see you this fine morning."

Foley wasn't as welcoming. "What are you doing here, Georgiana?"

He'd started growing a mustache since I'd seen him last, which gave me Tom Selleck *Magnum P.I.* vibes, except unlike Tom's luscious locks, Foley had no hair left on his head.

"What are *you* doing here?" I asked.

"We're checking out this bike."

I bent down to get a closer look.

"Don't touch it," Foley said.

"Why not?"

"Just … don't."

The bike was a light-pink Beach Cruiser with a brown wicker basket on the front, the perfect bike for riding along the coast. Except this bike had seen better days. The frame was bent, the front tire was flat, the chain was broken, and the wicker basket had a gaping hole in it. There were also small pieces of white paint flecks on some of the damaged frame and on the ground … along with what appeared to be dried blood.

A pastel sticker shaped like a rainbow was stuck to the back of the bike's seat. The words on the sticker read: *It's a good day for a good day.*

Kind of ironic, given the bike was having a bad one.

"Whose bike is this?" I asked. "Any idea?"

Foley and Whitlock glanced at each other and back at me. Foley crossed his arms, and Whitlock shrugged like he wanted to say more but couldn't.

"Oh, come on," I said. "I'll find out soon enough."

"I don't doubt it," Foley said.

"You're standing in front of a busted-up bike. There's what appears to be blood on the pavement surrounding it. The baggie in your hand contains a smashed-up cell phone. And Silas just parked behind me. Care to explain?"

Silas Crowe was the county coroner and a man I'd worked with for years. He hopped out of his VW bus, grabbed a rubber band off his wrist, and swooped his long, wavy hair into a man bun. He grabbed his camera off the seat and headed toward us, winking at me when we made eye contact.

"Nice to see you, Gigi," Silas said.

"And you, Silas," I said. "What are you doing here?"

"I'm, ahh … I'm not sure yet."

"I'm guessing there's a reason you drove over to take photographs."

Foley turned toward me. "Don't you have somewhere else to be? Like at your own place of business?"

"I'm in no rush."

He scratched the top of his forehead. "All right, fine. I'll throw you a bone if that's what it takes to get on with my day. We got a call this morning. One of the Remington girls never made it home last night."

"Are you talking about Rae's daughters?"

"I am."

"What happened?" I asked.

"That's just it. We don't know."

"What *do* you know?"

"When Dr. Rae arrived home last night, she checked in with her girls, as usual. Margot wasn't home. Her other daughter, Bronte, said Margot was out with a boy from school. Dr. Rae said her girls had a strict curfew whenever they were out, and Margot never missed hers. Dr. Rae showered, got into bed, and started reading, while she waited for Margot to arrive home. At some point, she fell asleep, and when she woke this morning, Margot wasn't home, her bed hadn't been slept in, and her bike wasn't in its usual place in the garage."

"When was the last time anyone saw Margot?" I asked.

"Bronte told her mother she'd had an argument with her sister yesterday afternoon," Foley said. "Afterward, Bronte went to her room and avoided Margot for the rest of the day."

"Does Bronte remember when Margot left?"

"She does not."

"What was the fight about?" I asked.

"I don't know," Foley said. "We haven't spoken to her yet. We were out looking for Margot this morning, and we came across the bike. It matches the description Dr. Rae gave us."

"Have you called the hospital?"

"Of course. Margot's not there."

"Does Rae know you found Margot's bike?" I asked.

"No, and I don't want you speaking to her about it."

He couldn't stop me from talking to Rae, a woman I considered a good friend. But for now, it was Foley's investigation, not mine, and I respected that.

There were far more questions than answers right now, and I couldn't help but wonder if something nefarious had happened to Margot. I wanted to believe there was a reasonable explanation for why she hadn't returned home. Still … Rae said her daughter never missed curfew. I assumed she'd have called if she were running late.

The mangled bike, the cell phone Margot had left behind, the stains on the pavement that looked a lot like blood … it all left me with an uneasy feeling.

A feeling I couldn't seem to shake.

3

Well, well, it's about time," Simone said when Luka and I entered the office.

She had a teasing tone to her voice.

Simone was wearing an Alice in Chains T-shirt beneath a black blazer and jeans. Our other partner, Hunter, was in a pair of overalls, but given it was December, she'd ditched her Birkenstocks for a pair of UGG boots.

"I got a little sidetracked," I said. "On my way to work this morning, I saw Foley and Whitlock standing on the side of the road, looking at a damaged Beach Cruiser. They believe the bike belongs to Dr. Rae Remington's daughter, Margot. She didn't come home last night."

"That's not good," Simone said. "Do you have any other details?"

"Foley said Margot had an argument with her sister yesterday afternoon. He doesn't know much more beyond that."

"Is there anything you'd like us to do?" Hunter asked.

"Not until we have more details. For now, she's a missing person."

"It seems odd that her bike was damaged and abandoned on the side of the road," Hunter said. "What about the hospital? Has anyone tried there?"

"Foley gave them a call. They haven't seen her. I noticed a couple of other things too—what appeared to be white paint flecks and dried blood around the area the bike was found."

"Maybe she accidentally ran into something," Simone said.

"There wasn't anything in close proximity to the bike that could have caused the kind of damage it sustained," I said.

"Hit-and-run, maybe?" Hunter asked.

"If it was a hit and run, you'd think the person who hit her would have left her there, but she was nowhere to be found," I said.

"I don't like it," Hunter said. "I don't like it at all."

Hunter's breathing had changed, a behavior I always tried to be aware of given she had panic attacks in times of high stress. She loved being a detective. She just preferred being behind the scenes, in the sanctuary of our office.

"Hunter, you okay?" I asked.

She stretched out an arm, which was covered in goosebumps. "I just … I don't have a good feeling."

"I know," I said. "I feel the same way. Until we know more, I say we lie low and allow Foley the time he needs to look into it. Let's keep an ear to the ground while he does. If anything even the slightest bit suspicious comes up about Margot, I want to know about it."

4

Margot had been missing for three days, which meant the odds of finding her alive were slim. Search parties had been formed, but so far, there was no sign of her. As the days folded into each other, there was an underlying sense of foreboding. Whispering around town occurred just about everywhere I went, with many residents speculating about what they thought had happened to Margot and why.

Over the last few days, Foley and Whitlock had knocked on doors and spoken to friends, neighbors, and classmates, trying to come up with a timeline for the day Margot went missing. So far what they knew was minimal.

Margot's sister, Bronte, told Whitlock she'd spent the first part of the day with Margot while their mother was at work. At around four in the afternoon, they'd made popcorn. Margot asked Bronte if she could borrow one of her sweaters to wear later that evening. It was then Bronte learned Margot planned to meet up with her ex-boyfriend, a fellow high school classmate named Sebastian.

Bronte claimed Sebastian had cheated on Margot at a party with another classmate named Kaia over the summer. Before long, the sisters' conversation became heated. Bronte didn't approve of Margot's plan to see Sebastian. Margot didn't care. She was seeing him anyway, whether Bronte approved or not. Frustrated, Bronte had stormed off, refusing to speak to her sister.

It was the last time Bronte saw Margot.

Bronte also stated she did not leave the house on the day of the argument, which meant there was a period of time before Rae arrived home when Bronte was alone, with no one to back up her story—a fact I found interesting. I had no reason to doubt her version of events, but it was in my nature to do so. I also wondered if there was more to Bronte's story, bits and pieces she may have left out.

Sebastian was next to be questioned. He said he planned on meeting Margot at a restaurant at half past seven. When he realized she was late, he sent Margot a text message, asking if she was still coming. When she didn't respond, he assumed he'd been stood up and that Margot was a no-show because she was still upset with him over his alleged infidelity.

There was over a three-hour gap of time between Margot's argument with Bronte and the time she was supposed to have met with Sebastian. And then a barmaid at the Untamed Shrew came forward to say she'd seen a girl matching Margot's description around six o'clock. The girl, if it was Margot, was walking from the boardwalk at Moonstone Beach toward the highway.

It made sense.

Bikes weren't allowed on the boardwalk.

I theorized Margot had left her bike somewhere, taken a walk along the boardwalk, and returned to retrieve the bike sometime later.

I was contemplating everything Whitlock shared with me when Dr. Rae walked through the office door, sniffling, and looking distraught. We locked eyes, and she slapped a hand to her mouth, hunching over as she burst into tears.

I rushed to her side.

"I'm so sorry, Rae," I said. "We all are."

"Thank you for the … for the … the flowers."

"I've been meaning to stop by," I said. "I knew you'd be inundated with calls and visitors, so I decided to wait. I should have come over. I see that now."

"It's all gone so wrong, so very wrong, and I just, I don't know what to do, and I can't … I can't …"

I draped an arm around her shoulder. "It's okay. Take a moment. Breathe with me. Okay?"

We spent the next few minutes doing breathwork, something I'd picked up from a spiritual guide I'd met at a wellness retreat.

Deep breath in.

Hold for count of four.

Deep breath out for the count of four.

It seemed to help.

As Rae became more relaxed, I walked with her to the sofa, and we sat down. Hunter rushed toward the kitchen, returning with a glass of water, which she handed to Rae.

"We don't need to talk about anything specific right now," I said. "We can just sit in front of the fire where it's quiet, and you don't have to deal with anyone calling or stopping by or pressing you with questions."

She nodded, and for the next several minutes, we sat in silent solidarity as she worked through her emotions. When the tears stopped flowing, she shifted her attention to a rock water feature at the far end of the office. It had been a gift from my fiancé, Giovanni, to celebrate the opening of the detective agency. It was a gem of a purchase, setting the mood for moments like the one I was sharing with Rae now.

Rae took a few sips of water and turned toward me. "I remember when you lost your daughter a few years ago. I thought I understood the pain you were going through back then. Now I realize I didn't have the first clue about what it must have felt like for you. I do now."

"It's one of those things you never wish on anyone. And hey, I know Margot hasn't been found yet, but most of the town is out there looking for her. We don't know what happened. Not yet."

I felt like a hypocrite as soon as I said it.

I'd just given her hope.

Maybe it was because I wanted to believe Margot would be found.

I just wasn't confident she'd be found alive.

Rae fisted a hand and pressed it to her chest. "The night Margot went missing, I assumed she had ended up coming home and was asleep in her bed. I woke up in the middle of the night feeling cold ... so cold, even though the heater was on, and the electric fireplace in my bedroom was going. I thought maybe I'd just had a bad dream. You know? I figured I'd wake up in the morning and everything would be okay. Except it's not okay, and the same frigid feeling I had is still there, living inside of me like an iceberg."

"Is there anything I can do?" I asked. "I want to help in any way I can."

"There *is* something, and it's the reason I'm here." Rae reached into her purse, took out an envelope, and handed it to me. "I want to hire you and your team. I want to know what happened to my baby, and I want ... I want ..."

The tears flared up once more.

I attempted to slip the envelope back inside her purse, but she set her hand on top of it, blocking me.

"I can't accept this, Rae," I said. "We're, well ... I consider you a good friend. It doesn't seem right."

"We are friends, and yet, *you* still pay when you come to my office. I will do the same."

"Are you unhappy with the way the investigation is going?"

"The first thing the police asked me was if I thought Margot had run away. To even consider such a thing ... it doesn't make sense."

"It's a standard question they ask everyone," I said. "It doesn't mean they think she ran off."

"Oh, they don't. They seem to think Bronte may have had something to do with Margot's disappearance. Can you believe it? As if we're not suffering enough already. They came into my home pretending like they cared, like they were on *our* side. In no time they began questioning Bronte and the statements she was giving. She didn't do anything. She's innocent. I need you to prove it, and I need you to find Margot. You'll help me, won't you?"

Foley was handling the investigation the way he should have been, but now wasn't the time to explain police procedure to her. Rae didn't understand how investigations were handled or how questions weren't just a way to get to the truth. They were also a way to rule someone out.

Staring at her now, I realized I would do anything to alleviate her pain, and I placed my hand on hers.

"I will help you," I said. "We will find out what happened to Margot."

5

W hy am I not surprised?" Foley stated.

I was sitting on a chair in his office, watching him pace back and forth.

"Rae's concerned you think Bronte is involved in Margot's disappearance," I said.

"She's right to think it. Truth is, I am questioning the girl's story."

"Why? What makes you consider her a suspect?"

Foley plopped down on his desk chair, opened a file folder, thumbed through some photos, and slapped one of them down in front of me. "See the big dent on the right side of the front bumper? Who do you think owns that car? Take a guess."

"Bronte?"

"Yep."

The car was light in color, but it wasn't white.

It had more of an ivory hue to it.

"What has Bronte said about the dent?" I asked.

"It took us a half an hour just to get her to talk about it at all. Then she admitted to hitting a car while she was parking at the grocery store. A *parked* car, mind you. Sounds like she was 'coming in hot' and lost control of the wheel."

"Have you spoken to the owner of the other car?"

"We have no idea who Bronte hit."

I crossed one leg over the other. "What do you mean?"

"Bronte left a note under the windshield wiper of the other car that said she was sorry. Then she fled the scene without talking to the other driver or reporting the incident."

"When did the fender-bender happen?"

"The day before Margot went missing, according to Bronte. Convenient, isn't it?"

"What did Rae say about it?"

"She didn't know about the damage to Bronte's car until I pointed it out. Bronte had been parking the car a little farther into the garage than usual, so her mother wouldn't notice it was dented."

"Bronte would have had to come clean at some point," I said.

"Maybe not. Her boyfriend works at an auto body shop. She said he was going to take care of it for her."

"Who's the boyfriend?"

"Daniel Moffat."

"Have you spoken to him?"

He nodded. "Daniel corroborated her story. Doesn't mean he's telling the truth. Doesn't mean she is either. The two of them could be in cahoots, for all I know."

"It's one thing to get into an argument with your sister. It's another to run her down while she's riding her bike."

Foley drummed his fingers along the edge of the desk. "Think about it. She could have been fuming after their argument, went for a drive, saw her sister on her bike, and decided to give her a little nudge. Maybe she hit her harder than intended. Maybe she hit her so hard that she killed her, and in her panicked state, she felt she had no other choice than to get rid of the body."

His theory, while having some merit, seemed a bit far out to me.

"It's … uhh, one way to look at it," I said. "Guess you'll know more after you examine the car."

"Silas is doing it now. Oh, and one other thing … when I spoke to the hospital, the nurse on duty the night Margot went missing said a man called and asked if they had a young woman by the name of Margot Remington there."

"I'm guessing the man didn't leave a name?"

"No, ma'am. The call came in around eight o'clock. That's all the nurse could tell me."

A man had been looking for Margot *before* she had been reported missing, a fact I found curious.

"Have you questioned anyone else about Margot's disappearance?" I asked.

"Several people. We just talked to Grant Nichols right before you arrived."

"Who's he?"

"Dr. Rae's boyfriend. Been seeing each other for about five months now. Likable guy. A lot younger than she is though."

Rae had kept Grant a secret. From me, at least. I wasn't bothered by it. She'd lost her husband a couple of years before. It made sense for her to take things slow with the new guy.

"How much younger is Grant than Rae?" I asked.

"About ten years."

Good for you, Rae.

"I wasn't aware she was in a relationship," I said.

"Grant told me Rae wanted to keep it quiet for the first few months for the sake of her daughters."

"Has he met Margot and Bronte?"

Foley nodded. "Last month."

"I wonder how they feel about their mother dating someone. As far as I know, Grant's the first boyfriend Rae's had since her husband died."

"I asked Grant how he's been getting on with them, and he said fine."

"*Fine?* He didn't elaborate?"

"He's just getting to know them. He's been out with search crews every day after work, looking for Margot."

It could have been because he cared.

Or there could have been another motive such as wanting to appear to look like he cared when he didn't.

"Where was Grant the night Margot went missing?" I asked.

"Driving home from work."

"In Cambria?"

Foley shook his head. "He lives in Templeton. Works there too."

The historic town of Templeton was about twenty-five miles from Cambria. Built in the late 1800s, it was named after the two-year-old son of the vice president of the Southern Pacific Railroad. For a time, the town was the end of the line for passengers traveling south, who often continued their travels by stagecoach to San Luis Obispo.

"Can anyone confirm Grant was in Templeton when Margot went missing?" I asked.

"His boss can't recall whether he saw him leave that day or not, but he said Grant almost always heads out at five on the dot. After my conversation with Grant, my gut feeling tells me he's not the type of person who'd do harm to anyone."

Having a gut feeling about a possible suspect after one meeting wasn't near enough to clear him in my book. And yet, Foley was quick to point a finger at Bronte. Until we knew more details about what had happened to Margot and why, it was too early in the investigation to separate fact from fiction, or to know whom to suspect.

"You're leaning on Bronte a bit too hard," I said. "There's no evidence she's not telling the truth."

"I lean hard on everyone, Georgiana. It comes with the job. You do the same."

"Have your suspicions if you want," I said. "But can you do me a favor and lay off her for now? Rae had a complete meltdown at my office about an hour ago. A missing child is a lot for anyone to go through, let alone a mother. You should know. You're dating my sister. You two hadn't met before her daughter, Lark, was kidnapped a few years back, but I'm sure she's spoken to you about what she went through."

Foley leaned back in the chair and gave me a look that said he hadn't just heard about the pain my sister had endured, he felt it, even now.

"I … ahh, I love that kiddo," he said. "I can't imagine anything happening to her."

"And Lark loves you. All I'm asking is for some compassion for Rae while we figure out what happened."

He went quiet for a time and then said, "All right. I'll do it as long as you agree to remain open to all possibilities. Rae may be your friend, but she didn't hire you to be her friend. She hired you to do a job—no matter where it leads in the end. Keep your eyes open, and I'll do them same. If you find out anything I should know, I expect you to call me."

6

Sebastian lived with his parents on a forty-acre mountaintop ranch with ocean views on one side and mountain views on the other. The estate was up for sale, boasting an eight-million-dollar price tag. From what I'd seen so far, it looked like it was worth every penny.

I entered the property through the open gate and drove up the dirt road leading to a grand cabin. Along the way I stopped to admire a herd of horses feeding beneath a magnificent oak tree in the distance. The picturesque scene looked like it was straight out of a painting. It was almost too beautiful to be real.

As I pulled up in front of the house, a good-looking, middle-aged man with whisps of salt-and-pepper hair peeking out from beneath a cowboy hat was unloading groceries out of the back seat of a souped-up black truck. He was dressed in a pair of jeans and a flannel button-up shirt with a vest over it.

I exited my car, and he turned toward me, squinting.

"If you're here for the open house, it's not for another couple of hours," he said.

"I'm here to speak to Sebastian," I replied.

He twisted the knob on the front door, set the groceries down in the entryway, and turned. "And who might you be?"

"My name's Georgiana Germaine. Rae Remington hired me to investigate her daughter's disappearance."

"What does Margot's disappearance have to do with Sebastian? They're not together anymore. Haven't been for some months now."

"They were supposed to meet the night Margot went missing. Were you aware?"

"According to my son, she never showed, so there was no meeting." He walked toward me and stuck his hand out. "I'm Sean Chandler, by the way. We were sorry to hear about Margot's disappearance. My wife and I took part in the search party last night. We plan to do the same tonight."

"Did Sebastian join in the search as well?"

Sean glanced at the cabin and leaned toward me, lowering his voice as he said, "My son … he, ahh … he's not doing so good. Hasn't left the house since we heard the news."

"If he cares for Margot, wouldn't he want to help look for her?"

"Well, of course he cares for her. We all do. I think he's just overwhelmed by it all."

"Do you know what happened between them?" I asked. "The reason they broke up, I mean."

"Are you referring to the night my son had a party while we were out of town?"

"I assume so."

Sean crossed his arms. "Look, there were a lot of rumors circling around after that night, a lot of different stories, most of them fragments of the truth but not the whole truth. In the end, we chose to trust our son's version of events. I'm inclined to believe he was straight with us, as he's always been."

It was something any parent in his position would say, and he'd said it with conviction, like he had no doubt. But did he? Or was he trying to convince me his version of the truth was the right one?

"Care to tell me more about what happened the night of the party?" I asked.

Sean smiled and said, "I do not, but I get why you'd ask."

"It would help if I could get a few minutes with Sebastian. And before you say no, I'm not here to make things harder on him, and I'm not accusing him of anything. All I'm trying to do is to find Margot. If I didn't think he might be able to help me in some way, I wouldn't be here."

Sean considered my request and said, "I tell you what, if you're willing to ask your questions in the presence of his mother and me, you got yourself a deal. I'm not sure he'll say much, but you can try."

Sean led me inside the house, showing me to the living room where I took a seat beneath a large chandelier made of antlers. A petite woman with long blond hair worn loose and cascading over her shoulders and down her back, walked in and sat on a chair beside me.

"I'm Meredith," she said. "Sean's in talking to our son right now. They shouldn't be long."

"I appreciate you both for the opportunity to speak with him."

Meredith crossed one leg over the other, bouncing it up and down as she said, "Can I ask you something?"

"Sure."

"How's Dr. Rae doing?"

"About how you would expect," I said.

"I'm so sorry about what she's going through. One of my gal-pals told me Dr. Rae hired you to help the police find Margot."

"I'm assisting the police, but yes. I'm also conducting my own investigation."

"Hmm."

Meredith leaned back, saying nothing for a time. "I hope you don't take offense to this, but why do you think Dr. Rae hired you when the police are already investigating it as a missing person's case? What can you do that they can't?"

Plenty.

She batted her eyelashes and had no doubt tried her best to form the question in such a way that sounded charming, but there was an underlying tone.

A tone which made me feel baited.

"Rae has her reasons for asking me to look into the circumstances surrounding Margot's disappearance," I said.

Meredith's face flushed. "I'm sorry. I shouldn't have said anything."

"There must be a reason why you did—a reason you're not sharing with me."

"You got me. You know how much people in this town like to talk."

"I do. What have you heard?"

She seemed delighted that I'd asked.

"Bronte and Margot had a fight the day Margot went missing, didn't they?" she asked. "I also heard Bronte may have been involved in her sister's disappearance."

"Who told you about the argument?"

"My son. One of his friends texted him. It's all any of his classmates are talking about."

"There's no evidence Bronte is involved."

Meredith raised a brow. "Oh, no? What about the dent on the front of her car?"

Good grief.

Word travels fast.

I wondered who had leaked it.

Perhaps Bronte's boyfriend.

"The police are following up on all leads right now, and so far, nothing points to any specific person," I said. "That's all I can say."

I could have said more, but I got the feeling if I did, it would go straight into her ear and out her mouth for all the town to hear.

"Again, I apologize," she said. "I didn't mean to be nosy."

Except she *had* meant to be nosy, and I was certain she wanted me to know it.

"It's fine," I said,

Meredith struck me as the type of woman who, even in her forties, was in a clique, where other ladies came together to keep up on the latest town gossip. I'd been invited into a few cliques in my time, but I'd steered clear of them. The last thing I wanted was to join an isolated group of hand-selected, pretentious ladies who excluded all those they didn't find worthy enough to be part of their circle.

Besides, I'd never been any good in groups that colored inside the lines. Coloring outside of them, on the other hand, had always made my life a lot more fulfilling.

"I hope y'all find Margot," Meredith said. "And I hope she's alive when you do. She's such a vibrant young woman. We just love her."

"My wife's right," Sean said, entering the room with a reluctant Sebastian in tow. "We were thrilled when Sebastian and Margot started dating."

"Why?" I asked. "What was so *thrilling* about her?"

"Let's just say we weren't always fond of the girls Sebastian chose to date before Margot came along," Sean said.

"Dad!" Sebastian said. "Stop."

Sean looked at me and shrugged like he didn't understand what he'd said wrong, and he took a seat next to his wife. Sebastian sat on the floor, crossed his legs, and started scrolling through his cell phone.

"It's nice to meet you, Sebastian," I said.

"Yeah, whatever," he said.

"I have a few questions for you. It won't take long."

"Yeah, well … I'm out here right now because my dad wants me to be, not because I want to talk to you."

"Sebastian, don't be rude," Sean said.

"It's okay," I said. "I'd feel the same way if I were him."

"Let's get this over with," Sebastian said. "What do you want to know?"

"The day you were supposed to meet with Margot, did the two of you communicate with each other?"

"We texted a bit."

"What did the text messages say?"

"I told her I was excited to see her. She said she was excited to see me too."

"What time did the text messages take place?"

Sebastian rolled his eyes, fiddled around some more on his phone, and then he handed it to me, a gesture I hadn't expected.

"Here," he said. "See for yourself."

Sebastian 10:10 am: *I can't wait to see you. I'm so excited.*

Margot 10:15 am: *I'm excited to see you too.*

Sebastian 1:10 pm: *Not long now. See you soon!*

Margot 1:11 pm: *Can't wait!* Heart emoji.

Assuming Sebastian hadn't deleted any other messages, the conversation ended there and didn't resume until that evening.

Sebastian 7:40 pm: *Where are you?*

Sebastian 7:46 pm: *Helloooooo?*

Sebastian 7:52 pm: *This isn't funny, Margot.*

Sebastian 7:57 pm: *If you're not here in five minutes, I'm leaving.*

Sebastian 8:02 pm: *Your loss. I'm out.*

There were no messages between the two of them after the last one I'd just read. I handed his cell phone back.

"I heard you and Margot had broken up a while ago," I said.

"I'm sure it's not something that's easy to talk about, but it would be helpful if I knew why."

Sebastian swished a hand through the air. "Man, I don't want to talk about it anymore. It's the past, you know? It's stupid. It has nothing to do with what's going on right now, so why does it matter?"

"I'm trying to learn as much about Margot and what she's like as I can from those who know her well. Any information you can give me would help."

"I don't see how. Nothing I tell you will help you find her."

I had plenty to say in response, but I decided to say nothing, to bite my tongue and see if he came around on his own. There was a moment of awkwardness, and we all sat there, staring at each other, and then Sean said, "I know it's hard, son. If you don't want to talk about it anymore, it's fine."

Thanks for the support, Sean.

I expected Sebastian to hop up and flee the room.

Instead, he looked at me and said, "Margot's the best. I've never met a girl like her. I can tell you one thing; she deserved a hell of a lot better than a guy like me."

Meredith gasped. "That's not true. You're a wonderful person."

"No, Mom. I'm not."

"Why would you say that about yourself?" I asked.

"Because of what happened, what I did. You know all about it. Don't you? Isn't that why you're here?"

"You're not being accused of anything," Sean said. "We wouldn't allow it if you were."

Sebastian ran a hand through his thick, curly, light-brown locks, and shook his head. "Margot was the best thing that ever happened to me. And I messed up. I messed up bad."

"Are you referring to the night of the party?" I asked.

He bit down on his lip and nodded. "Nothing would have happened if I would have just … if I hadn't gotten drunk that night. Maybe I would have remembered—"

"What *did* happen?"

"I don't know. It's the truth. I've thought about it so many times. I've tried hard to remember, believe me. I thought if I could, maybe I'd realize nothing had happened between Kaia and me, that it just looked like it had. We both had way too much to drink."

"Before you and Margot decided to meet up a few nights ago, had the two of you communicated since the breakup?" I asked.

"I texted her a few times. She didn't respond. I called. She didn't answer. She must have told Bronte I was trying to get in touch because Bronte passed me in the hall one day and shoved me into the school lockers. She threatened to jack me up if I didn't leave Margot alone."

"And did you leave Margot alone?" I asked.

"I did. It wasn't because of Bronte's stupid threat. It was because of what Bronte said. She told me Margot cried over our breakup almost every night."

"Who suggested the two of you get together—you or Margot?"

"Margot. She said she'd talked to Kaia and wanted to set things straight, since we'd never had a conversation about what happened the night of the party."

"What were you hoping would happen when you talked?" I asked.

"For a second chance, I guess. I would have done anything to get her back." He flicked a tear off his cheek. "I don't get it. Who would trash her bike? And where is she? Why is any of this happening?"

"I don't know, but I promise you this—I'm going to find out."

Sebastian looked at his parents and jumped to a standing position. He looked at me and frowned and then rushed out of the room, saying, "I'm sorry. I can't talk about this anymore right now."

7

Rae was sitting on a rocking chair on her front porch when I drove up. Standing on the steps a few feet in front of her was Bronte. The husky teenager's hair was in long, dark-blue pigtails, and she was dressed in black cargo pants with a silver chain looped around one of the pockets. Her matching shirt had a few rips in it, which looked intentional.

The more I stared at her, the more she reminded me of a cool, sassy, roller derby girl.

At present, Bronte was squinting, looking up and down the street like she was wary of any unwanted visitors who might stop by for a visit.

Her focus shifted to me, and she moved a hand to her hip.

"My mom's not seeing anyone right now," she said.

"Your mother is expecting me," I said.

"It's true," Rae added.

Bronte looked me up and down. "*You're* the detective?"

"I *am* the detective," I said.

"Huh."

I wasn't sure what about me was so off-putting, but something wasn't to her liking. This wasn't the first time we'd met, but she acted like she'd never seen me before.

I'm here, off-putting or not.

Deal with it.

Bronte moved to the side, allowing me to ascend the stairs so I could approach Rae. At the same time, the front door opened, and a man stepped out. He handed Rae a glass of wine, grinned at me, and said, "You must be Georgiana."

"I am."

"I'm Grant. Would you care for a glass of wine?"

I glanced at my watch.

Four o'clock.

Close enough.

It was my last stop of the day, after all.

"I'd love a glass," I said. "Thank you."

"Red? White? Rosé? Bubbles? We've got it all."

"Rosé, please," I said.

"I'll take a glass too," Bronte said.

Grant wagged a finger in her direction. "Nice try, young lady."

He turned and disappeared inside the house, but before he did, I noticed Bronte's sour expression was even worse than before.

She *wasn't* his biggest fan.

Then again, she wasn't a fan of mine either.

I decided to test the waters to see if I could elicit a response.

"Grant seems nice," I said.

"He is," Rae said. "He hasn't left my side since we found out Margot was missing."

Bronte rolled her eyes. "He doesn't need to be here twenty-four seven, does he? I'm here, Mom. I'm all you need."

"I appreciate you," Rae said. "I appreciate Grant too. You've both been wonderful."

Grant returned with my glass of rosé, and Bronte made for the front door.

"Hey, Bronte, can I talk to you for a few minutes before you go inside?" I asked.

She blew out a long sigh and said, "Why?"

"You know why," Rae said. "Georgiana's here to help."

"One of the reasons your mother hired me is to help take suspicion off of you," I said. "In order to do that, I need to know a few things."

Rae stood and placed a hand on Grant's arm. "We should give Georgiana a moment with Bronte alone."

"You're leaving me?" Bronte asked.

"I'm not *leaving* you. I'll be right inside. I've known Georgiana for a long time. I trust her. You can too."

Rae followed Grant into the house, leaving the disgruntled teen at my side.

When the front door closed, I said, "How are you holding up?"

"Oh, well, let's see. How would you be holding up if the fight you had with your sister caused her to leave and now she's missing?"

"Fair point."

"Are you here to question me like the cops did?"

"I am not," I said. "I'm here to talk."

Her cell phone buzzed. She read the message on the screen, muttered a few swear words, and slid the phone into her pocket.

"Do you need a minute?" I asked.

Ignoring the question, she said, "I can't believe he has the nerve to reach out to me right now."

"Who texted you?"

Her gaze dropped to the floor, and she shrugged. "No one."

"Does 'no one' have a name?"

She leaned against the house and blinked at me. "You remind me of … I don't know, a parrot maybe."

I took it as a compliment.

"Parrots are one of the most intelligent birds," I said. "I've been compared to worse in my day."

The quip struck a chord, and she burst out laughing.

I laughed too, and for the first time since I arrived, she smiled instead of scowled at me.

"Love the vintage clothes, by the way," she said. "And your car's sick. What is it?"

Compliments from a teenager.

I felt like I'd struck gold.

I didn't speak teenager well, but I'd heard 'sick' was the new version of 'cool.'

"The car's a '37 Jaguar," I said.

"What's it worth?"

Cheeky question.

Then again, she seemed to be the type of girl who never hesitated to speak her mind. And while we were from different eras, something about her reminded me a little of myself when I was her age.

"The car is priceless," I said. "It was my grandmother's. She left it to me when she died. And I'll leave it to … well, my niece I suppose, one day."

"Why your niece? You don't have kids?"

"I had a daughter. She passed away."

Bronte pressed a finger to her lips. "Oh, sorry. I shouldn't have, you know—"

"It's all right. Are you older or younger than Margot?"

"One year older. So, what are the odds my sister is going to be found alive at this point? You can be straight with me. I've looked up the statistics. None of it is good."

"I tend not to focus on odds or statistics. I prefer to take each situation as it comes. But you're right. The outlook isn't great at this point."

"I think about it a lot, the fight we had the other day. I think about what I could have said instead of what I did. Who argues over a stupid sweater? It's so lame."

"The argument wasn't about a sweater, was it? It was about Sebastian."

She crossed her arms, huffing, "I couldn't believe she agreed to see him after what he did to her."

"Do you know for a fact Sebastian did what he was accused of that night?"

"Yeah … I mean, no, but—"

"Sometimes in life, we see things the people we're closest to don't. In those times, as much as we want to shake some sense into them, I've learned what they want the most is support. I'm sure Margot had her reasons for wanting to meet with him."

"I guess."

"No matter what you said to her a few days ago, what's happened isn't your fault."

"It *is* my fault. You can say it. It's what everyone thinks. Hell, the cops think I ran her over with my car. And then what? I tossed her into the ocean or something so I wouldn't get caught?"

Her bottom lip was trembling. She bit down on it, forcing herself not to cry.

"This is where I come in," I said. "I don't believe you had anything to do with Margot's disappearance. Let's shift the focus from you to the person who's responsible."

"How?"

"Tell me more about Margot," I said. "What's she like?"

"I see what you're doing."

"What am I doing?"

"Talking about her like she's still alive. If you think it will help me feel better, it won't."

"I'm not trying to do anything except have a conversation."

She stared at me a moment and said, "We don't argue, not a lot. We're complete opposites. She's soft, and I don't mean that in a bad way. She's easy to love. Sometimes I wish I was more like her."

"In what way?"

"When we were kids, if she wanted attention from my parents and she wasn't getting it, she'd give it to them first, hoping she'd get it back in return. It always worked. I couldn't … I mean, I've never been good at that kind of thing. I don't know why."

"I was the same way growing up. Initiating contact felt unnatural to me, I guess."

She nodded. "Yeah, you get it. Margot is the most likable person I know. Guess it's what makes this all so bizarre."

Bronte's phone buzzed again.

She looked at it, shouted more expletives, and hurled it onto the grass.

"You sure you don't want to talk about it?" I asked.

"It's Sebastian. He wants to meet up somewhere to talk. What does he think? We're gonna get together and have a kumbaya bonding moment because my sister's missing? Freaking idiot."

"I stopped by his house earlier today and talked with him."

She moved a hand to her hip. "What did he have to say for himself?"

"His concern about your sister seems genuine."

"It's not. It's an act."

"You don't believe he cares for your sister?" I asked.

"Sebastian and I used to work together at the grocery store. We became good friends. He was assigned to work with Margot on a school project a while back, and after that, she was all he could talk about. He told me he wanted to ask her out. I'll be honest, it was weird for me. But I stepped aside, and I allowed him to date her. And then I watched her get destroyed by him because he couldn't keep it in his pants."

She'd *allowed* him to date her.

Interesting choice of words.

It was almost as if she was saying if she hadn't wanted them to be together, they wouldn't have been.

"Were you upset when Sebastian told you he liked Margot?" I asked.

"Are you asking if I've ever had the hots for him or something? No, I haven't. He's nowhere near my type … too cookie-cutter clean."

Now seemed like the perfect time to switch subjects.

"Do you remember what Margot was wearing the last time you saw her?" I asked.

"I already gave a full description to the police. What, you all don't get together and share stuff?"

"We do, sometimes. Other times, I'd say we're guilty of keeping things from each other."

"Why?"

"I don't know. I suppose we have our reasons."

"Do you trust them—the cops in this county?"

"I do. I know Chief Foley well. He's dating my sister. He's a good guy who just so happened to have forgotten to tell me what Margot was wearing when she went missing."

Bronte shook her head at me, like she could see straight through my ploy to bring her back around to the question she still hadn't answered.

"Margot was wearing a white sweater, brown pants, and pink-and-white tennis shoes," Bronte said. "Anything else you want to know?"

"I need to ask you about the incident with your car," I said. "It's not because I think there's any merit to the idea that you had something to do with Margot's disappearance. I need to make sure I have the facts—all of them."

Bronte blew out a heavy sigh. "About the car … I should have handled it better. I know what I did was wrong."

"I'm not passing judgment here. What's done is done. I just want the details."

"All right. I was thirsty, so I decided to stop at Sea Breeze Market to grab a drink. I found a parking spot, and right as I was getting ready to pull in, this bird swooped down to grab a piece of food on the ground. I swerved, trying not to hit it, and I ran into the car in the next parking spot over instead."

"What happened next?"

"I got out and checked the other car for damage. It was just a scratch. I figured the owner might not even notice it. My car was the one that got dented."

"Why did you leave a note?" I asked.

"I don't know. I felt bad."

Not bad enough to remain at the scene.

No passing judgment, Georgiana.

Remember?

Easier said than done.

"What did you say in the note?" I asked.

"I wrote, 'I'm sorry. I may have scratched your car.'"

"That's it?"

"Yep."

"And you didn't sign your name? Leave a number? Nothing?"

She shook her head, pursed her lips.

"And you left right after?" I asked.

"I did."

"What did the other car look like?"

"It was red. A Civic, I think, or maybe a Corolla. It had a few other scratches and dings, so I thought, it's not like it was in pristine condition … you know, before I nicked it."

Way to justify what she'd done.

Judgmental much?

At least I wasn't saying what I was thinking out loud.

"Thanks, that's all I need to know about the accident," I said.

"Are we done? It's freezing out here."

"I have one last question … What do you think about your mom's boyfriend?"

"Grant? I don't think anything about him except how nice it would be if he went home."

"Earlier, it looked like you were irritated with him."

"Ever since we met him, he's tried to step in, play the father role. He's never raised any kids, and he has no clue how to be a parent. If he wasn't here, my mom would be fine with me having a glass of wine. I'm eighteen. In my opinion it's close enough to twenty-one."

"Have you talked to your mom about Grant?"

She shifted her focus, looking through the window at Grant and Rae, who were talking to each other in the kitchen.

"I've never said anything about him to her," she said. "He makes her happy. And it's not like I'll be here much longer. I'll be off to college soon."

"What do you know about Grant?" I asked.

"Not much. I've never tried to—"

The front door opened, and Rae said, "Grant just finished making dinner. We're grabbing a quick bite before we head out to join the search party. Georgiana, you're welcome to stay."

The aroma of sauteed garlic and fresh bread wafting onto the front porch smelled divine.

"I appreciate the offer, thank you," I said. "Giovanni's cooking for me tonight."

"Another time then."

"Sure."

Bronte headed inside, turning around before she closed the door to say, "Hey, thank you … you know, for being here for us. It's nice to know someone has our back."

I sat next to Giovanni, picking at the delicious food he'd made with my fork. I was trying my best to be in the present moment, but my thoughts were all over the place.

"What do you think about us buying a vacation home in Italy, spending part of the year there and part of the year here?" Giovanni asked.

"Yeah, sure," I said. "Wait, what?"

I glared at him, and he laughed.

"It's good to see I have your attention," he said. "You haven't responded to a thing I've said in the last few minutes."

He was right, and I felt awful about it.

"I'm sorry," I said. "You deserve for me to be focusing on you, and all I'm thinking about is this case."

"Is it the case, or is it the fact you're not joining in on the search tonight?"

The original plan had been for us to eat dinner together and then meet up with Simone and search for Margot. A half hour earlier, plans changed when Hunter called. To my surprise, she suggested I take the night off.

With few leads to pursue at this point in the investigation, Hunter had decided to join Simone in tonight's search. Being on the front lines of the investigation instead of behind the scenes was the kind of thing that gave her anxiety. Tonight, she'd decided to push herself out of her comfort zone, and I was proud of her for it.

I'd wanted all of us to search together. But as I thought about why Hunter suggested I stay behind, I figured it was because she wasn't sure how she might react to being "out there" instead of huddled behind a computer. If she had a panic attack, I assumed she wouldn't want me to see it, even though I would have understood.

Above all, Hunter preferred to keep to herself, including all her quirks. At least as much as possible. And based on some things she'd said over the years, I got that her introverted ways was a protective shell of sort, so that she wouldn't "let me down"—as if she ever could. So, out of respect for her, I'd bowed out on the search, but after I did, I called Simone. She promised to keep an eye on Hunter tonight for any signs that she might be struggling.

Simone's assurance should have been enough to ease my mind, but it wasn't.

"I feel scattered," I said. "One minute, I'm thinking about how Hunter is doing. The next, I'm thinking about what everyone said to me today. The next, I'm worried we won't ever find Margot."

Giovanni reached over and took my hand in his. "How many times in the history of your investigations have you not solved one of them?"

"Zero."

"So what are the odds you won't this time?"

"Zero, I guess?"

He smiled. "Three feet of ice does not form in a single day."

Ever since we'd met in college, he sprung Chinese proverbs on me from time to time. He always knew the right thing to say and the right way to say it.

"You're right," I said, blowing out a sigh. "Sometimes I just expect answers before I even know what questions to ask."

He leaned in and gave me a kiss. "I know what you need."

"And what's that?"

"A nice, long soak in the hot tub. It's the perfect night for it."

Given it was winter, nothing appealed to me more than slipping into a hot tub of water while the cool, coastal breeze washed over my face.

"I'm in," I said.

"Good. I'll clear the dishes. You go ahead and get a head start."

"You will be joining me, right?"

"As soon as I can. My sister called right after you arrived home. I was finishing up dinner at the time, so I waited to return the call."

"Tell Daniela I said hello," I said. "And remind her she promised to come for a visit."

"Will do. I won't be long."

I changed clothes, the pitter-patter of Luka's paws scampering alongside as I stepped out onto the back deck and lowered myself into the hot tub. For the first time all day, it felt like I was starting to relax.

I leaned back, my eyes fluttering closed as I struggled to stay awake.

When my eyes opened, I was no longer in the hot tub. I was in a wooded area, and I was cold—freezing cold—and soaking wet, like I'd just gone for a swim.

I ran my hands up and down my goose-fleshed arms and noticed I was still wearing the swimsuit I'd had on in the hot tub. I was also barefoot, and when I took a step forward, my foot came down on a twig. The twig snapped, and a sharp pain shot up my leg.

Looking around the fog-laden area, I saw no one, but I heard a symphony of noises. Trees blowing in the wind, shifting and bending to its will. Screeching owls somewhere in the distance. Insects buzzing. And something, or someone, behind me.

I turned, blinking into the darkness as I said, "Hello? Is someone there?"

"Hello," came a soft, melodic reply.

"I can't see more than a couple of feet in front of me. Where are you?"

"I am here."

"Here where?"

"Everywhere."

"Where are we?" I asked.

Laughter echoed around me.

"You tell me," she said. "It's your dream."

"Margot?"

"You didn't search for me tonight."

There it was—the underlying guilt I'd been feeling all evening. The feeling that I wasn't doing enough. It was never enough. *I* was never enough. One of the many lies I chose to tell myself, even though I knew better than to believe it.

"Everyone is looking for you," I said.

"Everyone except you. You don't know where to look, do you?"

"I don't."

"Why not?"

Because of reasons I didn't want to say out loud.

Saying them out loud made them seem true.

"Because I want you to be alive," I said. "For Rae. For Bronte. For you."

"What's happened has happened. There's no turning back now. You can't change the past. All you can do is seek the truth."

"You're dead, aren't you?" I asked.

"Are you sure about that?"

"I am."

And I was.

"How are you sure?"

"I don't know," I said. "I feel it. I felt it since the moment I laid eyes on your bike."

"Allow your feeling to be your guide."

"You had plans to see Sebastian the night you disappeared," I said.

"There were things I needed to say that he needed to hear."

"What things?"

"The truth. I wanted him to know he could trust me."

"Sebastian was the one who broke the trust with you," I said. "Wasn't he?"

"Trust goes both ways, doesn't it? There are those in your own life you don't trust. Wouldn't you agree?"

I wanted to lie, but I didn't.

"I suppose I don't trust anyone," I said. "Not all the way."

"Why not?"

"I believe there are sides to all of us, sides we don't show to anyone else."

"Have you ever shown anyone all of your sides?"

"I try," I said.

"Don't you think it's time you tried harder?"

"I do, and I will. Tell me how to find you."

"You should know by now it doesn't work that way."

"Point me in a direction. Any direction."

Silence.

"Are you still there?" I asked.

Silence.

"Hello? Margot?"

"I run in the woods by day. At night, I sit, but you will not usually find me alone. My tongue sticks out and waits to be filled in the morning. What am I? What am I, Detective Georgiana Germaine?"

A hand brushed across the side of my neck, and the dream came to an end.

My eyes flashed open.

Giovanni was standing just outside the hot tub, a look of concern on his face.

"Are you all right, *cara mia*?" he asked. "Did you fall asleep?"

"A shoe," I said.

"A shoe?"

"She's a shoe."

"Who's a shoe?"

"Margot. I was with her just now. Well, not *with her* with her. I was having a dream. I couldn't see her, but I talked to her. In my mind, at least."

He stepped into the hot tub and sat beside me. "Tell me about it."

I considered what Margot had said, or perhaps what I'd said to myself, about trying harder to show everyone who I am. If anyone deserved all of me, it was him. It had always been him.

I told Giovanni everything I could remember.

When I finished, he said, "Do you have any idea where you were?"

I shook my head. "I couldn't see more than two feet in front of me."

"Why do you think she told you the riddle?"

"I don't know," I said. "It surprised me."

"Did anything else about the dream stand out to you?"

Recalling the short encounter I'd had with Margot, I said, "There was noise all around me. It sounded like I was in the forest."

"Good, anything else?"

"I had a hard time pinpointing where Margot was because of the thick, gray fog. It was everywhere."

"I wish I would have known you were dreaming," Giovanni said. "I would not have disturbed you."

"It's all right. Most of the dreams I have like this don't last long anyway. Who knows what any of it means, if anything."

Giovanni smiled and looked me in the eyes. "I believe we're at the point where you can admit some of the dreams you have are unique in their own way. You believe there's something to these dreams. If you didn't, you wouldn't have bought the book about empaths that's sitting on your nightstand."

He was right.

I'd had too many dreams over the years to deny the fact that while most of my dreams were nothing out of the ordinary, some were far from it.

Maybe Margot was trying to tell me something.

Now I just needed to find out what.

I woke the next morning to the sensation of someone touching me. I looked up and saw Giovanni hovering over me, his hand running up and down my arm.

"How did you sleep?" he asked.

"Not bad," I said.

"Any more dreams?"

"Not about Margot."

He nodded and said, "Come, there's something you need to see."

I pushed the comforter to the side and followed him over to the balcony door. He opened it, and I stared out into the foggiest, rain-filled morning I'd seen in a long time.

"In the dream you had last night, you said it was foggy and you were wet," he said.

"I did. How do you feel about going for a drive?"

He grinned. "I'm glad you asked."

I changed into a pair of denim overall dungarees, which always gave me Rosie the Riveter vibes when I wore them, and black, knee-length, waterproof boots fit for hiking the trails during winter. I searched the hall closet for my rain jacket and met Giovanni at the door.

"Where shall we go first?" he asked.

I considered places similar in terrain to the one in the dream I'd had, but there were far too many.

"Let's start in an area no one has searched yet," I suggested.

Ever since Margot was reported missing, Foley had set up search parties using a grid system. It began in town and worked its way out. His system was perfect, but so far, they'd come up empty-handed.

We headed out of town, until we came to the first trail that hadn't been searched yet.

We parked.

We searched.

We found nothing.

We drove to another trail.

We parked.

We searched again.

Still nothing.

The fog continued to roll in. The rain was falling in sheets now, making the chances of finding Margot slim, my hopeful mood burning out by the second.

Giovanni remained upbeat, saying, "Even if we don't find anything, I'm glad you asked me along this morning."

I grabbed his hand and gave it a squeeze. "Thank you for being, you know … you."

"Thank you for being *you*," he repeated.

As we walked back to the car, my spirits lifted, and my motivation to keep looking returned. We agreed to make one last stop. If we found nothing, we'd quit for now, head back to town, and have brunch at the Boathouse Diner. The diner had an old brick fireplace in the back room, the perfect spot to cozy up and warm my frozen digits.

The next trail we stopped at did a full loop, meaning it could be hiked at the start of the trail from either side. I went left, and Giovanni went right.

About a quarter of the way around, a snapping sound echoed in the distance, and I stopped, cupping a hand over my eyes as I took in my surroundings.

"Giovanni?" I called.

I received no response, and I didn't expect I would. Even if he'd walked the trail faster than I had, he wouldn't have made it this far around already. I picked up the pace, heading in the direction of the sound I'd heard. Several feet in front of me, I spotted a man wearing sunglasses, a black hoodie, and jeans. He had the hood pulled over his head and a headlamp strapped around it. He was holding something in his hand, but I couldn't make it out.

"Hey!" I shouted.

The man froze for a second.

Without turning around, he abandoned the trail and took off into the woods.

I was wet, cold, and tired.

Too tired to chase after him.

But I did.

It wasn't long before I realized he was a lot faster than me. With each passing moment, he seemed to get farther and farther away, until he made a foolish mistake. He turned to see how far away I was, and in doing so, he tripped over a log, faceplanting onto the ground.

My luck, it seemed, was changing.

I took a deep breath in and sped toward him. I was still several feet away when he managed to get back on his feet. He attempted to flee a second time, but the obvious injury he'd sustained to his left leg made it difficult. Instead of running from me, he limped, giving me the opportunity to grab him from behind, tackling him to the ground.

I ripped the sunglasses from his face, and I realized the man I assumed I'd been chasing was a teenager—a teenager I'd met before.

And that wasn't all.

When I forced him to the ground, the item he'd been holding in his hand fell to the ground, and I gasped, my eyes locked on a woman's pink-and-white tennis shoe.

S ebastian?" I asked. "What are you doing here?"

He looked up at me and grunted, "I could ask you the same thing."

"Answer the question."

"Screw you, lady."

Giovanni, who'd just caught up to us, bent down, his face inches from Sebastian's as he said, "You will speak to Georgiana with respect. If she asks you a question, answer it. Do anything to the contrary and your leg won't be the only injury you sustain this morning."

Sebastian looked at Giovanni and then at me. For a moment, it appeared like he might make another snide remark, but he stopped himself. Instead, he cleared his throat and said, "I've been looking for Margot every night since I found out she was missing."

"Your parents told me you haven't left the house in days," I said.

"They have no idea. I've been slipping out after they go to bed."

"Why not join the search party like everyone else?"

He sat up and tried to wipe the dirt off his jeans, which didn't work.

"I don't feel like seeing or talking to anyone from school right now," he said. "My cell phone's been blowing up. I just want to be left alone."

"You say you want to be alone, but you texted Bronte yesterday, didn't you?" I asked.

He blinked at me, shocked I knew he'd reached out to her. "I … uhh, yeah. I figured she's dealing with the same thing right now. If she agreed to meet up, I was going to tell her what I've been doing the last few nights and see if she wanted to search with me."

"Did Bronte text you back?"

"No."

He reached for the shoe he'd dropped, and I stood in front of it, blocking him. "Leave it where it is for now."

"I can't."

"You can, and you will," I said.

"You don't understand."

I understood a lot more than he realized.

"You mind telling me why you're out here, walking around with a woman's shoe in your hand?" I asked. "Looks to me like it's the same shoe Margot was wearing the day she went missing."

"I found it," he said.

"Where?"

"I didn't find anything else, if you're wondering. Just the shoe."

"*Where?*" I asked.

"I'll show you. It won't matter. Like I said, there's nothing else to see."

"When did you find it?"

"Maybe an hour before the sun came up."

"It wasn't light yet," I said. "It's possible you missed something."

"I searched the entire area with my headlamp. I was worried, you know? Worried I might find her right by where I was …"

He tried to finish the sentence, but his emotions got the better of him, and he choked on his words.

I gave him a moment to collect himself and then pointed at the shoe. "Do you recognize it?"

He nodded.

"Is it Margot's?"

He nodded.

"Are you sure?" I asked.

"We … ahh, we were hanging out at the mall one day about a month after we started dating. She saw a pair of tennis shoes she wanted in the store window. She was going to save up until she could buy them. After I dropped her off at home that night, I went back to the mall and bought the shoes as a surprise. She wore them almost every day, even after we broke up."

I bent down, inspecting the shoe.

"It has no laces," I said. "Looks like it could slip right off her foot."

"It happened sometimes. She didn't care. She loved 'em."

"You said you search for Margot at night, while your parents are in bed, but they'll be awake by now. They must know you're not at home."

"Every night before this, I've made sure to get back before the sun came up. After I found the shoe this morning, I didn't want to stop looking."

"Have you spoken to your parents yet?" I asked. "Do they know you're here and what you've found?"

"They know I'm here. My mom has been texting me, wanting to know updates and when I'm coming home."

"What did you tell her?"

"I said I'd be back soon."

"When you realized the shoe you found was Margot's … well, first off, you should have left it there. You've tainted a potential crime scene. And second, why didn't you call the police to report your findings?"

He crossed his arms and sighed. "Call them and say what? I'm out here by myself with no alibi, and I just so happened to find my ex-girlfriend's shoe. Do you think they would buy it? I wouldn't if I were them."

His response seemed a bit suspicious to me, and based on the look on Giovanni's face, he agreed.

If Sebastian had nothing to hide, admitting he'd found Margot's shoe wouldn't matter.

"What was your plan?" I asked. "Were you going to take the shoe home and not tell anyone about it?"

He threw his hands in the air. "I don't know. I don't have a plan. I should have called the cops, okay?"

"You do realize it's too late now, right?" I said. "I'll have to call it in."

"Fine, call it in. You can tell them *you* found it. There's no reason to involve me."

"Not happening. You *are* involved."

"Who cares who found it? What difference does it make?"

The kid had a lot to learn about how things worked—about how *I* worked.

"It's better to be honest from the start," I said.

He wiped his nose and said, "I guess you're okay if they arrest me, then? I've done nothing wrong."

"What makes you think you'll be arrested?"

"Aside from the bike they found, the shoe is the only other evidence they'll have. They'll lock me up. I know they will."

"As long as you're telling the truth, you have nothing to worry about," I said.

"You don't know that."

Except I did.

His parents were loaded. If Foley so much as hinted about arresting Sebastian, his parents would make plenty of noise.

"I'm sure your parents have a great lawyer," I said.

"They do."

"Is there anything else I need to know, anything at all?" I asked. "If there is, now's the time to tell me."

"I've answered all of your questions, haven't I?"

"You answered my questions because you had no other choice."

He shot a glance at Giovanni and said, "Yeah … well, your bodyguard threatened me."

Giovanni tipped his head back and laughed. "Bodyguard to the famous Detective Georgiana Germaine. It has a nice ring to it."

I shook my head and slipped my backpack off my shoulder. I unzipped it and riffled inside for a pair of gloves and a large Ziploc bag. Doing what I could not to touch more of the shoe than I had to, I dropped it inside the bag and slipped it into my backpack. Then I turned toward Sebastian, offering him my hand.

"Come on," I said. "It's time for you to show us where you found the shoe."

11

Given Sebastian's trip-and-fall over the log earlier, I wasn't sure how well he'd be able to walk. It turned out he was fine. Just a few minor scrapes and a potential bruise that would manifest later. He'd found Margot's tennis shoe beside a large boulder nestled beneath a grove of towering pine trees. As I walked around the boulder, I called Foley, telling him what had been found and where we were. I used my phone to drop him a pin to our exact location, and while we were on the call, he rounded up Whitlock and a couple of others and said he'd be on his way in no time.

While we waited, Sebastian stood off to the side, talking on the phone to his father. The call ended, and Sebastian said his parents were en route and would join us soon. I hoped Meredith had enough wits about her to keep quiet and not alert the entire town about what her son had found. It was wishful thinking, at best, but we needed time to check out the area before everyone started swooping in.

The trail we were on wasn't far from town. While we waited for the others to arrive, we continued searching. The fog had lifted, and the sun was peeking through the clouds. I hoped a second glance would yield positive results.

As it turned out, I was in luck.

Dangling from a branch not far from where the shoe had been found was a strip of torn fabric. The fabric was dark blue and appeared to be made of cotton. The color wasn't a match to any of the clothing Bronte said Margot was wearing the day she went missing. But what if it was a piece of her abductor's clothing?

I took a few photos and left the fabric strip undisturbed, noting its location so we could circle back once Foley arrived.

The torn cloth was about fifty feet away from the tennis shoe, which seemed to tell its own story. Perhaps Margot escaped her attacker and was chased into the forest. The shoe could have slipped off, and the assailant, in hot pursuit, had clipped a branch in his desperation to capture her, thereby leaving behind a piece of his clothing.

Giovanni tapped me on the shoulder and pointed toward the trail. Whitlock and Foley were walking in our direction. Whitlock was dressed like he was headed to Sunday brunch in a paisley shirt with a black leather jacket over it, fitted black trousers, and his signature thick, black eyeglasses. Instead of the polished shoes he often wore, he had on hiking boots, a sharp contrast to the rest of his attire.

Whitlock approached me and winced, bending down to rub his ankle.

"Is everything all right?" I asked.

"Oh, yes," he said. "I'm as chipper as an old chap sipping on a pint at a pub on a Sunday night. Might need to get rid of these shoes, though. Pity, I just bought them."

"I take it you're not used to wearing hiking boots."

"No, ma'am. Never owned a pair of hiking shoes in my life. Not until Miss Margot went missing."

"Don't give up on the new boots yet. Give yourself a little time to break them in."

He leaned toward me and whispered, "After we find Margot, I'm donating these rugged beauties to Goodwill. I have no use for them."

"I'm guessing you're not the outdoorsy type," I said.

"If by outdoorsy you mean sipping a margarita in a cabana by the pool, I'm as outdoorsy as they come. If you're talking about climbing Mount Everest, not so much."

Foley shook his head and said, "Are you two just about finished? Because I'd sure like someone to show me where the shoe was found."

Sebastian lifted a finger. "I can help you there, sir."

"*Sir*?" Foley scoffed. "That's 'Chief Foley' to you, kid. I assume you're the idiot who removed the shoe from where you found it?"

Sebastian nodded. "I am the idiot, and I'm sorry."

"Do you need a lecture about why you don't move potential evidence during a police investigation, or has Georgiana reprimanded you already?"

"I know what I did was wrong," Sebastian said.

"Good. You're still getting a lecture from me, but I'll save it until I get the chance to talk to your parents."

Sebastian looked at me like he was worried he might be arrested right then and there, and I mouthed, *Don't worry, it's going to be fine.*

In the distance, I noticed Silas had arrived, along with Officers Higgins and Decker, who hung back on the trail. I wondered why they weren't joining us, and it soon became evident when I spotted Sebastian's parents. Once they reached Higgins, he held a hand up, stopping them from stepping one foot in our direction. It was a plan I assumed Foley had put into place before they arrived—a smart decision on his part. Until we knew what we had or didn't have, it was better to keep the public at bay.

Silas made his way over to us, shook hands with Giovanni, and glanced at me.

"Mornin', Gigi," Silas said. "I hear you have a shoe for me to look at."

"I do."

I grabbed the bagged shoe out of my backpack and handed it to him.

"What do you know about it?" Silas asked.

I tipped my head to the side and said, "This is Sebastian. He's Margot's ex-boyfriend. He recognized the shoe as one in a pair he bought for her when they were together."

Silas acknowledged Sebastian with a nod and held the baggie up, staring inside.

"Huh," he said. "It isn't the type of shoe someone would forget, now, is it? Where was it found?"

"We were just about to make our way over to where the kid discovered it," Foley said.

The six of us, which included Foley, Whitlock, Silas, Sebastian, Giovanni, and me, walked toward the boulder. Silas took photos, while Whitlock and Foley milled around, inspecting the area around it.

"There aren't any visible tracks," I said. "I already looked. I'm guessing if there were, the rain we've had this week has washed them all away."

"Guessing so," Foley said.

"There's not much more to see here by the looks of it," I said. "Not around the boulder anyway."

Foley placed a hand on Sebastian's shoulder. "I see your parents have arrived to collect you. You should join them."

"Are you saying I can go home?"

"You can … *after* you go to the police department and answer a few questions. I'm only going to say this next part once: I want this kept quiet. If what's been found gets out before I have a chance to get on top of it, I'll know who to blame. We have a lot of ground to cover, and we need time to cover it. That goes for you *and* your parents. Understood?"

Sebastian nodded.

Once he was out of earshot, Whitlock nudged me. "What do you think? You believe the kid's story? You think he was just out here, searching for the girl, and happened to stumble upon her shoe?"

"I don't know," I said. "I'm not saying he's guilty of murder or anything, but something doesn't feel right. He could have planted the shoe for all we know."

"Seems guilty, if you ask me," Whitlock said. "I mean look at him. Reminds me of that old folk tale about Henny Penny. Has a look in his eyes, like any second now he expects an asteroid to hit, bringing the world to an end."

If Sebastian cared for Margot like he said he did, part of his world *had* come to an end.

"Show me the piece of fabric you found," Foley said.

"It's over here," I said.

We huddled around the strip of material, and Foley took his notebook out of his pocket and began reading the things he'd jotted down over the past couple days.

"Let me save you some time," I said. "Margot was wearing a white sweater, brown pants, and pink-and-white tennis shoes the last time she was seen."

"Mmm … what do we make of the piece of fabric?" Foley asked. "Is it an item unrelated to her disappearance, or could it have gotten torn off someone else's clothes—someone who was with her the other night?"

It was more of a question he was asking himself than one he expected me to answer.

Silas clipped the branch off the tree and bagged and tagged the snippet of fabric.

"Doesn't appear to have any stains on it of any kind—no blood," Silas said. "Then again, there's not much to it."

Foley ran a hand along his chin. "What to do now … I need to make some calls. I'd like to get a couple more officers out here to help us look around. Georgiana, I'd like you to remain, if you don't have anything pressing."

"I can stay," I said. "I just need to eat something. You don't want me fainting on you out here."

"No, I do not."

"I'll go into town and return with food for everyone," Giovanni said.

Foley tipped his head toward Giovanni. "Much appreciated. And hey, you're welcome to join in the search when you return, if you like."

"Of course. I'll assist in any way I can."

"Good. It's settled." Foley turned toward me. "Reach out to Simone, would you? Let's get her out here too. I'd also suggest Hunter, but she had a bit of a hard time during the search party last night."

"In what way?"

"Jittery, like she was struggling to be there. Nothing too bad. Still, it's my impression she might not be up for it right now. Would you agree?"

"I would," I said.

Based on what we'd already found, who knew what else we'd discover today?

F oley mapped out our individual search locations and instructed everyone to meet back in a couple of hours to report our findings, or lack thereof. A half hour into my search, I came upon a creek. I stopped at the water's edge, listening to the soothing murmur of the water as it slid and tumbled over rocks and crevices. Glancing at my hands, I realized they were in desperate need of a wash. I crouched down, immersing them into the icy water before shaking them off in the chilly afternoon air.

The forest area adjacent to the trail was brimming with sights and sounds. Birds chirped from above, and the occasional bend and snap of twigs and branches crunching could be heard in the distance. The view was breathtaking, and yet, it was often in the most magnificent and tranquil of places that my mind wandered the most. It wasn't long before I was thinking about how easy it would be to hide a body here—a body that, if hidden well enough, might never be found.

As I pondered the thought, the sun's rays filtered through the trees, casting light onto the terrain. My eyes came to rest on the forest floor on the opposite side of the creek. A bit of ground looked different than the area surrounding it—ground which appeared to have been disturbed. If not for the thickets of leggy weeds rising up around it, I may not have even noticed the difference in terrain.

I hunched over, eyeing the depth of the creek. I guessed it was about a foot or two deep, and at most, twenty feet wide. I rolled my pants, stuck my boots into the water, and trudged my way to the other side. As I stepped out, a sound in the distance startled me, and I turned, scanning the area I'd just come from.

Whitlock was seated on a rock, his face forlorn as he stared down at his hiking boots like he wanted to chastise them. He removed both shoes, and his socks, and plunged his feet into the creek. Closing his eyes, he bellowed out a sigh of relief.

I felt sorry for him, imagining the pain he was feeling. Even so, I couldn't contain my laughter. It echoed around me, and he peered across the creek, forcing a smile as he said, "Well, well … fancy meeting you here."

"How bad is it?" I asked.

"If you're referring to the numerous blisters I've acquired, it's possible I'll need to be hauled out of here on a stretcher before day's end."

"I'm glad you decided to take a break. If you keep going, your blisters will get worse."

He lifted a finger. "Good point, except for one thing: I'm no quitter."

"Don't think of it like you're quitting. Think of it like you're looking after yourself. I always carry a first aid kit with me. I have ointment and some bandages, if you're interested."

"Once I've given my feet a bit of a soak, I'd be most grateful. How have you been faring this fine afternoon? Anything noteworthy to share?"

I expected nothing less from Whitlock.

Even in pain, he still found a way to remain positive.

"Before I crossed the creek, I was standing right about where you are now," I said. "When I looked over to this side, I was sure I saw some terrain that looked a bit different from the rest. Now that I'm over here, I can't seem to locate it."

"Is there anything I can do to help?"

"Stay where you are. I don't want to add any additional wear and tear on your body today."

He pulled off his glasses, wiped them off on his shirt, and slid them back on again. "Speaking of wear and tear, I should have changed into more hiking-appropriate clothing before coming out here. There wasn't time."

"Do you even own any hiking-appropriate clothing?" I asked.

"Come to think of it … *no*. I do not."

We had a good laugh, and as our laughter died down, I continued my search. I walked several feet away from the creek and froze. I had been right. The soil beneath where I now stood was soft and crumbly, unlike the hard ground around it.

Had a hole been dug and covered over?

It sure looked like it.

If I was right, the digger had done a shabby job.

I reached into my backpack, grabbed a pair of gloves, and slid them over my hands. Then I turned toward Whitlock, cupping my hands to the sides of my mouth, shouting, "I think I found something. Someone may have dug a hole over here."

"How big?"

"From the looks of it, big enough to dispose of a body."

"You're checking it out, right?" he asked.

"I don't see any reason why I should wait. Do you?"

"I don't. Could be nothing. Could be something. Why not find out?"

He had a point, and it was my find, after all.

I crouched down and pressed my fingers into the soil, using them as a trowel to scoop and shift dirt around.

One foot down—nothing.

I kept going.

Another six inches—still nothing.

Another couple of inches, and something brushed across my glove that didn't feel like soil. I bent down to get a better look and jerked my hand back, standing, as I shouted to Whitlock, "I found something!"

"Something good?"

"Good enough that we need to get Foley over here right now."

13

I t all started with a finger. A finger attached to an arm, attached
to a dead body … Margot's body. In an instant, the search for the
kindhearted teen had come to a tragic end, the heart-wrenching
truth bearing down like a gut punch to the chest.

A few facts were apparent:

Someone had murdered her.

Someone had dug a shallow grave.

And someone had put her in it.

Why here, less than a quarter mile away from a popular trail,
and not somewhere else?

Maybe her murderer hadn't planned anything out before he'd
taken her.

Maybe he panicked.

Perhaps Margot had broken free from her captor somehow. She
ran, and he chased after her. He caught up to her, and he killed her.

And there was something else, something inside the grave that
was even odder. The white sweater Margot was last seen in had been
folded in half and placed with precision over her face, almost like it
was done with consideration and care.

Why would the killer bother?

Perhaps he planned to return, to visit her again.

As we huddled around the burial site, we stood silent, taking a moment to honor her life.

Silas removed a few tools from his kit, and while we waited for the rest of his team to arrive, he gave us instructions on how we could assist him in the meantime. It wasn't long before the sun dipped behind the mountainside, the daylight ebbing with each passing moment.

My thoughts turned to Rae and Bronte—and how much I'd hoped for a different outcome than the one presented to us now. There was nothing easy about a mother losing a child in this manner, and there never would be. Now would be a time of grief, a time of pain, but one day I hoped Rae and Bronte would find a way to heal.

As I stared down at Margot's battered and broken body, I felt rage rising inside me. The lit match of justice flicked onto the kerosene, fueling my desire to catch the person who'd committed this heinous crime and make them pay.

Foley bent down and wiped his eyes.

"Horrible," he said. "It's just horrible. What kind of an animal does a thing like this to a young woman?"

"Or to anyone, for that matter," Whitlock said.

"This all started with the bicycle accident," I said. "What I'd like to know is ... was it, in fact, an accident, and the person who ran her down did a snatch-and-grab to avoid facing charges? Or had she been taken on purpose?"

"Once she's examined, I hope we have the answers to those questions, and more," Foley said. "For now, it's been a long day."

"I agree," I said.

Foley stood up again, facing everyone who remained. "I want to thank all of you for your efforts today. The forensics team will be arriving any moment now. I'll hang back until they get here. The rest of you can go on home."

I didn't want to go on home.

I wanted to stay, to see what more was unearthed as Margot's body was lifted from its resting place.

Silas and I exchanged looks, and I felt certain he knew what I was thinking. He gave me a nod that said, *Don't worry. I'll call you when I know something.*

For now, that would have to be enough.

Turning toward Foley, I said, "I need to talk to Rae."

"Yeah, I know," Foley said. "Now that we have a positive ID, it's the right thing to do. But I'd sure like to keep a lid on things until tomorrow. Small town like this … who knows how everyone will react?"

"The way they always do," I said. "Every time something like this happens, they come together in unity and support."

"Margot's young. I suspect once word gets out, a wave of anger will ripple through town, citizens seeking their own vigilante justice, pointing the finger at anyone and everyone they suspect could be involved."

"It might be a good call to hold a press conference sooner than later," I said. "I've always found when people are informed, and they believe they're not being lied to and that they can trust what you're telling them, they're a lot more willing to keep the peace."

Foley crossed his arms and sighed. "Yeah, I guess you're right. Talking to the press isn't my strong suit. Always feel like I never say the right thing."

"I'll be alongside you the whole time, if you like," Whitlock said. "I can even step in and make a comment or two."

"I just might take you up on that," Foley said. "You have a way with words, and people. A natural charisma. Everyone likes you."

Whitlock beamed at the compliment.

Foley returned his focus to me. "I should be the one who talks to Rae and Bronte, but since she hired you to investigate, and I'd like to remain here for a while, you go on ahead and speak to her tonight."

I'd decided I would be speaking with Rae either way, but knowing I had Foley's approval made my job even easier.

"And … uhh, it almost doesn't seem right for me to have you ask her to keep the news quiet for now, but would you anyway?" he asked.

"I will. Speak to you soon."

14

called your office several times today," Rae said, hands on her hips. "Hunter assured me you'd get back to me as soon as you could. That was eight hours ago."

I reached out, taking Rae's hand in mine. "I know, and I'm sorry. Can I come in? We need to talk."

"Why? What's happened?"

We locked eyes, and for a moment, no words were spoken between us. It was as if she'd just realized why I'd stopped by so late and why I hadn't been in touch before now. She released my hand, shaking her head as she leaned against the front door for support.

"No, no, no, no, no ..." she said.

"I'm so sorry, Rae. I wish I didn't have to be the one to—"

She held up a hand in front of her.

"Stop. Just stop. I don't want to believe it." She looked down the hall, toward the kitchen. "I made Margot's favorite dinner tonight. It's sitting at her spot at the table, ready for her when she gets home. I keep telling myself she's still coming home, and that she's all right, and that we'll be together again as a family."

I didn't know what to say, so I said nothing.

Knowing Margot wouldn't return home for a meal tonight or any other night wasn't something she was ready to hear yet.

Rae swayed from side to side, her legs buckling beneath her as she began sagging to the floor. I reached out, pulling her into my arms. An onslaught of tears followed, and for several minutes, I didn't move. I just stood there, holding her, wishing I could do more, but knowing nothing I could do or say would ease her anguish.

I felt like a failure, even though I wasn't sure what I'd failed at—maybe bringing Margot back home, alive—making the impossible possible?

I wondered if Bronte was at home, or Rae's boyfriend, Grant.

If they were, I assumed they would have heard us by now.

After some time, Rae regained her composure and pulled back from my embrace.

"Where is she?" she asked. "Where is my daughter?"

"We don't have to go over the details tonight, Rae," I said. "I can come back tomorrow, first thing, if you want. There's no rush."

Rae shook her head. "I need to know. I'm going to find out anyway. It may as well be now."

"We should sit down," I suggested.

I followed Rae into the living room, taking a seat next to her on the sofa.

"I feel so empty," she said. "It's like all the air has been sucked out of my body. I can't eat. I can't sleep. I was sitting out on the front porch earlier and a bird landed on the porch railing. It perched there for the longest time, blinking at me. It was almost as if I could have reached out and touched it, and it would have allowed me to do so. I almost started talking to it if you can believe … like the bird was Margot. Sounds crazy, right?"

"No, it doesn't," I said. "Not to me."

She took a deep breath in and said, "What have you come to tell me?"

"This morning, Giovanni and I decided to do some searching for Margot on our own. New areas. We stopped off at a few trails, and we were unsuccessful, and then we came across Sebastian."

"What was he doing on the trails? I heard he's been staying inside, not wanting to see or talk to anyone."

"According to him, he's been sneaking out at night, after the search parties have finished for the evening," I said. "He claims he's been looking for Margot."

"And do you believe him?"

"I don't know what to believe. When I found him, he was holding a shoe in his hand. When I got a closer look at it, I realized it matched the description of the ones Margot had been wearing the day she disappeared."

"Why would Sebastian have Margot's shoe?"

"He told me he'd found it in the same area we were searching. He showed me where, and I called Chief Foley. Foley came out with a handful of people from the police department. We split up and started searching. I was standing beside a creek, and I noticed a patch of dirt that looked different than the surrounding area. I walked over to check it out, and that's when I … when I started digging and … I umm, I found—"

Rae slapped a hand over her mouth. "It was you? *You* found my baby girl?"

"It was me, yes."

She threw her arms around me and said, "Thank you."

The last thing I felt I deserved were words of appreciation. But I understood why she'd offered them. All too often missing persons were never found, leaving a gaping wound where loved ones couldn't heal. And while the outcome wasn't what any of us wanted, Margot could now be put to rest.

"She's dead, isn't she?" Rae asked.

"Yes, I'm sorry, Rae."

I heard what sounded like someone descending the stairs, and I turned to see Grant standing at the bottom of the staircase with nothing but a towel wrapped around his waist. Eyes wide, he looked at me like he was shocked to find me there.

"I apologize," he said. "I didn't know anyone else was here."

While we hadn't been loud, I assumed our voices had carried enough for him to know Rae was talking with someone inside the house. Then again, if he had heard her talking, he could have assumed she was on the phone.

He pivoted, speed-walking back up the stairs.

I wondered if Grant had ever walked around in a towel in front of Margot and Bronte. I was about to pose the question to Rae, and I noticed she was looking at me funny, like she wondered why I had an inquisitive look on my face.

No point hiding my concerns now.

"Does Grant walk around in just a towel often?" I asked.

Rae shook her head. "Good heavens, no. Never, unless we're in the bedroom together. It was just supposed to be us for most of the night. Bronte's out. We don't expect her home for a couple of hours, at least."

"Is she with her boyfriend or other friends?"

Rae shook her head. "I should have told you earlier."

"Told me what?"

"Bronte's with Sebastian Chandler."

Sebastian Chandler.

The guy got around.

The last I'd seen Sebastian, he'd joined his parents and was going down to the police department for questioning. I wondered what had come of it.

"I thought Bronte and Sebastian weren't speaking to each other," I said.

"They weren't. He sent her a text message earlier today. I don't know what it said. She didn't tell me. All I know is that it was enough for her to decide to meet up with him."

I wondered if Sebastian had told Margot about the shoe he'd found. He'd been asked to keep quiet about it, but it didn't mean he would be.

"When can I see Margot?" Rae asked.

"They're still processing the area where she was found," I said. "It will take some time. They want to make sure they don't miss anything."

"I want to see her for myself. Will you take me?"

"They're not allowing anyone at the scene right now."

"I'm not *anyone*, Georgiana. I'm her mother."

"I know. And I know how hard it is to wait, but we need to give the police and the forensics team the time they need to gather evidence."

She frowned, disappointed with my answer.

"You're asking a lot of me … too much," she said. "How would you feel if you were in my position?"

Years earlier, I *had* been in her position.

She clasped a hand over her mouth as if she realized what she'd said the moment the words left her mouth. "Oh, Georgiana. I'm sorry. I wasn't thinking. I wasn't thinking about—"

She wasn't thinking about my daughter, Fallon.

"There's no need to apologize," I said.

She grabbed a tissue from a box on the coffee table and leaned back, crossing one leg over the other as she blotted her eyes. "Do you know what happened to Margot? Do you know how she died?"

"I don't, not yet. I'm good friends with Silas, the county coroner. He'll get in touch with me once he's had the chance to do a thorough examination. As soon as I know something, you will too. You have my word."

"How long will it take? Any idea?"

"Silas is tireless on cases like this one. He'll work into the night if it means getting us the answers we need sooner."

As more tears began to fall, Rae reached for a few more tissues.

"I just want to be by her side, you know? Even if she's no longer here, with us, she needs her mother."

I squeezed my hands together, swallowing back tears of my own.

Now was not the time for me to fall apart.

Rae needed me—she needed me to be strong.

"Who else knows about Margot?" she asked.

"As far as I'm aware, we've managed to keep it quiet so far. Chief Foley doesn't want it to be talked about until he's able to inform the community. I assume that will take place tomorrow."

"Are you asking me not to speak of it until then?"

"I'm not here to tell you what to do, and I won't," I said. "I'm just passing along his wishes. And they have merit."

The front door opened, and Bronte sprinted toward her mother. Sebastian trailed behind, his hands shoved in his pockets, eyes darting around, focusing on anything other than the two of us.

"They found Margot's shoe, Mom!" Bronte said. "Can you believe it?"

It wasn't until Bronte had blurted it out that she noticed me sitting there.

She wagged a finger at me.

"*You*. What are you doing here? I thought you were out with the others, searching for my sister." Bronte turned toward Sebastian. "That *is* what you said, isn't it?"

"You should sit down, honey," Rae said.

"I don't want to sit down. I want to know what the detective is doing here."

Rae looked past her daughter and said, "Now is not a good time, Sebastian. You should go home."

Sebastian looked at Rae and then at me.

"You're here because you found her," he said. "You found her, didn't you?"

I held my gaze on Sebastian but said nothing.

A wide-eyed Bronte said, "Is he right, Mom? Have they found her?"

"Bronte, I think it would be best if you—"

"Don't do this, Mom!" Bronte said. "Don't drag it out! Just tell me the truth."

It was clear Sebastian wasn't leaving without an answer, and Bronte wasn't about to let up, either, until she heard the truth.

Grant dashed down the stairs, his eyes laser-focused on Bronte, and he said, "Don't you ever speak to your mother like that."

I gave Grant a look that I hoped would compel him to say nothing more.

It wasn't *his* place to interfere.

Bronte wasn't his daughter.

"Are you freaking kidding me right now, Grant?" Bronte said. "Don't you dare tell me what to say or not to say. Who the hell do you think you are?"

"I'm your mother's boyfriend," Grant said. "She's going through a lot right now, and the last thing she needs is you coming in here and upsetting her."

"I've been through a lot too," Bronte said.

"We all have," Grant said. "This isn't just about you."

Oh, Grant.

Shut up.

Quit before you make it worse than you already have.

Bronte clenched her fists and stepped toward the man. "You shouldn't be here. You're not family."

Grant reached out, grabbing Bronte's shoulders, and shaking her. "Now you listen to me, kid …"

Sebastian started walking toward them.

I stepped in front of him and faced Grant.

"Take your hands off Bronte right now," I said through gritted teeth.

Grant should have heeded my warning, but he didn't.

Instead, he said, "She's upsetting her mother."

"Stop it, Grant," Rae pleaded. "Please. You're making things worse."

"Don't you see what she's doing, Rae?" Grant said. "Don't you see how she treats you? How she talks to you? I can't stand for it."

And I couldn't stand for his mitts being on Bronte any longer.

I grabbed one of Grant's arms, wrenching it behind his back as I clamped my other hand on the back of his neck, thrusting him down the hallway. He tried to resist, but I persisted. I got him out the front door and gave him a shove. He tripped, falling over himself.

Looking at him now, I could admit that I'd shoved him a skosh harder than I'd intended, but Grant didn't have much meat on the bone. He was lucky I hadn't done worse.

I closed the door behind me and reached out a hand, offering to help him up.

He refused to take it, which came as no surprise.

"You need to leave," I said.

"I think you broke my arm."

He sounded like a whiny child.

"No, I didn't," I said. "It's sprained, at best. It's not my fault you tripped over yourself."

"I tripped because *you* shoved me."

"I gave you a chance to take your hands off Bronte. You didn't listen. You're not a child. You don't get a warning and a count of three before I act."

He pushed himself to a standing position and backed against the wall of the home, leaning over, panting. "I should call the cops on you. You assaulted me."

"And *you* assaulted Bronte. So, yeah, go for it. I'd love to explain to the police how you put your hands on a teenage girl, a girl who *isn't* your daughter."

"I didn't hurt her. She's fine."

He wasn't getting it.

"You have a temper," I said. "Is this the first time you've put your hands on one of Rae's daughters, or have you done it before?"

He rolled his eyes. "Stop. I've had enough of your questions. I would never do anything to hurt Margot or Bronte. We may not always see eye to eye, and I suppose part of the reason is because I'm not used to being around teenagers."

He turned away from me, his breathing growing heavier by the moment.

"Even if you haven't raised kids before, you understand right from wrong," I said. "It was wrong to grab Bronte the way you did."

One minute passed, then two, and his breathing steadied.

"I was just trying to talk some sense into Bronte, that's all," he said. "She can be a lot to handle. Rae doesn't need any more stress in her life."

I stood there, staring at him, wondering how honest he was being with me.

I needed to know more about this guy.

I needed to know *everything*.

"Rae's been through a lot tonight," I said.

"What's happened?"

"I can't talk about it yet. If I could, I'd tell you. Ask me tomorrow. Right now, Rae needs some time alone with her daughter."

"It's Rae's decision to make."

"Perhaps, but I've just made it for her. If you care for her as you say you do, give her some alone time tonight with her daughter. Go home and call her in the morning."

"What about Sebastian? He's still here."

"Sebastian will be leaving too," I said.

He reached into his pocket and pulled out a set of car keys, using the same arm he'd alleged I'd broken. I marveled at his speedy recovery and almost laughed out loud as he looked at me, then his arm, and realized why I was smiling.

"I ... ahh, I left my iPad at home and was going to go and get it anyway," he said. "If I agree not to come back tonight, will you give Rae a message for me?"

"Sure."

"Tell her I'm sorry, and I'm here if she needs me, no matter what the hour."

An apology for Rae, but no apology for Bronte.

That, in and of itself, was telling.

15

I reentered the house, and Rae and Bronte had their arms around each other in a tight embrace. Sebastian was sitting on the floor, his legs crossed, head slumped over—sniffling.

I gave Rae the short version of my conversation with Grant, and then I pulled Bronte to the side, asking her to give me a call if Grant showed up before morning. She agreed, and I walked over to Sebastian, tapping him on the shoulder.

"Come on," I said. "I'll walk you out."

Without looking at me, he nodded.

When we got to his vehicle, I said, "What did Rae tell you?"

"Nothing much. But you're here, and I can tell by the way she's acting that Margot's dead. She must be."

"Chief Foley is trying to keep it quiet until tomorrow," I said. "It would be a big help if you could keep your assumptions to yourself until then."

"I won't say anything."

"Not even to your parents?"

"Not tonight. I just want to be alone."

"Foley asked you to keep quiet earlier, yet you told Bronte about the tennis shoe."

He shrugged. "Sorry. It … slipped out."

"If you get the urge to talk to anyone else, you can talk to me."

He shook his head. "You think I'm a suspect. Why would I talk to you?"

"I think everyone is a suspect. It's my job. I believe you loved Margot, which means you should have no problem supporting me in doing whatever I need to do to find out what happened to her and why. It's like I told you earlier, if you're innocent, you have nothing to worry about."

He rubbed his hands together and pressed them to his lips, blowing on them like he was trying to keep warm.

"I've been thinking about the other night, about how mad I was when Margot didn't show up," he said. "I should have been there for her. Maybe if I was, none of this would have happened, because I would have been there to protect her when she needed it most."

I placed a hand on his shoulder. "Don't put this on yourself."

Not unless you're guilty.

"Too late," he said. "I already have."

He opened his truck door and slid onto the seat, but instead of starting it up, he sat there, making me wonder if there was something more he wanted to say.

"Is there anyone else you think I should question?" I asked. "Anyone at school, or someone Margot talked about in the past? Anyone who was a problem for her in any way?"

"I'd have to think about it. She wasn't the type of person who had enemies."

"What about Kaia? Is she still interested in you?"

"Kaia? Nah. She's dating someone else now. Besides, she's always felt bad about what happened the night of that stupid party. She never wanted to break us up. She wasn't even interested in me. After the party, when we talked, she said …"

He leaned back for a moment, not finishing the sentence.

"She said *what*, Sebastian?" I asked.

"I'm sure it's nothing."

"If it's nothing, there's no reason you can't share it with me."

He went silent for a time and then said, "Kaia remembers bits and pieces from that night, just like I do."

"Is there a *bit* or a *piece* you'd like to share?"

"Maybe one thing. Kaia told me someone opened my bedroom door during the party, letting her into my room where I was on the bed, passed out."

"Who let her into your room?"

"I don't know."

"Guy or girl?"

"A guy. Since she's new here, she didn't know his name. She tried to describe him to me, and he sounds like every other guy I'm friends with, so … Anyway, she swears the guy told her he wanted to play a joke on me, and he asked her to go along with it."

"What kind of joke?"

"He said she should tell me she was Margot just for fun. But I mean, even if she's right, why would someone do that? It's messed up. The guys who were at the party are all my friends."

Friends.

It reminded me of a quote from Shakespeare's *As You Like It*.

Most friendship is feigning, most loving mere folly.

I could think of one deceptive reason a friend would pull such a prank—perhaps someone wanted the relationship between Sebastian and Margot to end.

But whom?

And why?

16

The next morning, I called Hunter and asked her to gather whatever information she could on Grant Nichols. Then Simone and I grabbed coffees at 2 Little Figs. We talked about Kaia and what Sebastian had said about the night of the party. Since school was out for Christmas break, Simone offered to stop by Kaia's house to see if she could speak with her. We parted ways, and I headed over to the coroner's office to check in with Silas.

It was quiet when I walked in, which was unusual. Most days, eighties hair-band music could be heard before I even entered the building. Looking around, I didn't see anyone at first. It wasn't until I walked into Silas' office that I found him sitting on the floor atop a plush cushion. His eyes were closed, and through the speaker on the phone at his side, a woman on a YouTube channel was leading him through guided meditation. Not wanting to disturb his session, I took a step back, the heel of my shoe scraping against the polished lab floor.

Silas opened one eye and jerked his head up, looking at me.

I raised a hand and said, "Hey, I didn't mean to disturb you."

"Are you kidding? It's because of you that I gave guided meditation a try. It's cool. I like it, though I think I may have fallen asleep toward the end."

"How long have you been meditating?" I asked.

"A few weeks. You were right. It helps me focus. Well, most days. This week, it's been a struggle. This case is taking up a lot of space in my mind—too much, I think."

It wasn't often Silas was rattled the way he seemed to be now.

It had me worried about what details had come to light during Margot's examination.

"I'm a bit off today myself," I said. "Seems like you are too."

"Is it that obvious?"

"Your eyes are bloodshot, and you look like you haven't slept in days."

"Except for the quick catnap I just had, I haven't."

"Do you want to talk about it?" I asked.

"Let's start with the good news. We finished processing Bronte's car. The paint is not a match to the flecks we found scattered on the ground where Margot's bicycle was located."

It was a relief, and it didn't surprise me.

"And the bad news?" I asked.

He squeezed his eyes shut, his head shaking back and forth. "It's bad, Gigi."

"How bad?"

He opened his eyes and looked at me. "Margot was … she was raped. In my opinion, at least. It's hard in cases like this one. I based my assessment on the condition her body is in and what I discovered during my examination."

She was raped.

I stood a moment, letting it set in, wanting to believe it wasn't true, that there was some other explanation to rationalize his findings.

"What can you tell me?" I asked.

Silas moved the cushion to the side, grabbed his phone, stood up, and walked to his desk. "Best I start from the beginning, after you left us last night."

"All right."

He sat in his office chair and leaned back, tapping a finger to the desk, thinking.

I sat across from him.

"It took a couple of hours to dig her body out of the shallow grave she'd been put in," he said. "When we were able to get a good look at her, the first thing we noticed, besides the careful folding of her sweater over her face, was that she was wearing a tank top and a bra … and nothing else."

We already knew Margot had been wearing a sweater the day she went missing. The tank top must have been underneath it.

"What do you mean by 'nothing else'?" I asked.

"She had no panties and no bottoms of any kind. She had socks on both feet, and she was wearing one sneaker, which was a match to the other one Sebastian found."

"Was there any other clothing in or around the burial site?"

Silas nodded. "A pair of brown pants were laid out beneath her body."

Similar to the sweater. It seemed so odd, almost like she had been staged or placed there with a level of consideration postmortem.

But why?

"Can I take a look at the crime scene photos?" I asked.

"Of course. I should warn you … I know you've seen plenty of homicide photos over the years. Even so, these might be tough for you to look at, given your friendship with Rae."

"I still need to see them."

"I figured as much."

Silas grabbed a file folder out of the top drawer.

"I'll start off easy, show you the ones I took of the pants first," he said.

He thumbed through the photos, pulled a few from the stack, and handed them to me. I stared at them for a moment, taking it all in. The pants Margot had been wearing were positioned at the bottom of the shallow grave with such perfection, it was obvious extra time had been spent to arrange them in such a way.

It puzzled me.

The killer could have done anything with those pants. He could have balled them up and tossed them into the hole. He could have burned them in another location. Or he could have taken them and disposed of them later.

And yet ... he hadn't done any of those things.

"Strange," I said. "Who kills someone and then takes the time to arrange the pants the way they did?"

"Good question."

My mind swirled with thoughts about the killer's psyche that night. When killers covered their victims, it often indicated an emotional attachment, like the killer was familiar with the victim. In this instance, it was almost as if he felt some remorse for what he'd done.

"I assume Margot had injuries?" I asked.

"She did. Several in and around the genital area, including a lacerated wound on the wall of her vulva. There was also a significant amount of bruising around the genital area. I also found bruises on her wrists, suggesting she was held down at some point by her assailant."

Silas pulled several more photos from the stack and handed them over. I struggled to get through them, each one contributing to the story that led to the end of her life.

He was right.

Based on the position of the bruising, all indicators pointed to rape.

I leaned back in the chair, closed my eyes, and laced my hands behind my head, trying to recreate what I believed had happened that night.

Margot was struck by a vehicle while riding her bike, after which she was abducted and driven to the hiking trail, which would have put them there right around nightfall. Given she'd lost one of her shoes, a shoe located in a separate area from the place she was buried, I believed my initial idea about her attempting to flee and get away from her attacker was right. At some point she lost a shoe, but she kept on running. She made it all the way across the creek before he caught up to her, forcing her to the ground and raping her.

But how had she died?

"Have you established the cause of death yet?" I asked.

"Blunt force trauma to the side of the head."

"Using what?"

"Based on her injuries and where she was found, I believe it was a rock or something similar. There are a couple of possibilities."

"Meaning?"

"The most probable cause of death is murder."

"Most probable?"

"I can't rule out the idea that Margot may have tripped, fallen, and hit her head, which could have contributed or led to her death."

"Did any of the rocks in the surrounding area have blood on them?"

He shook his head.

"I also scraped beneath her fingernails," he said.

"And?"

"I found blood and skin cells. It's possible she scratched the person who attacked her."

I sat there, trying to work out the scenario Silas had just presented. Had Margot been injured first and then raped and murdered? Or had she been raped first and somehow managed to flee afterward? Whether she'd died because of an accidental injury or by her attacker's hand, the fact remained … she was dead.

There were still a lot of questions to be answered, but we now had several key details:

Margot was hit by an automobile.

She was taken to a trail just outside of town.

She was raped.

She died by way of accident or she was murdered in cold blood.

"Can I see the rest of the photos?" I asked.

Silas bit down on his lip, reluctant to hand them over, but he knew I wouldn't budge until he gave them to me. I spread them out over his desk, taking my time going through them. Now and then, I'd pause and look away when the graphic nature of the photos was too much to bear.

Once I finished, I stacked the photos together. As I handed them back, a wave of nausea came over me. I clasped a hand over my mouth and ran to the bathroom, where I spent the next several minutes crying into the toilet as I emptied the contents of my stomach.

I remained there for some time, breathing in and out, until I was able to gain a modicum of control over my emotions. When I opened the bathroom door, Silas was waiting outside, leaning against the wall with a glass of water in one hand and a couple of tablets in the other to help soothe my stomach.

"You were right," I said. "Looking at those photos was a lot harder than I figured it would be. I can't remember the last time one of my cases affected me this way."

He placed a hand on my shoulder. "It's understandable. We all love Dr. Rae."

"All I could think about when I was looking at the photos was how I was going to bring myself to tell her what happened to her daughter."

Telling Rae that Margot was dead was one thing.

Telling her the way in which she'd died was another.

"I know she's your client, but you could always have Foley or Whitlock speak to her if it's too hard," Silas said.

He was right.

I could.

But I knew I wouldn't.

17

'd just entered the office and taken a seat next to Hunter on the sofa when I noticed she was staring at me like she was about to burst.

"It looks like you have something you want to say," I said.

"Grant Nichols was accused of sexual assault," she blurted.

I sat up straighter. "When?"

"It was a while back. He was twenty-two at the time."

"How old was the girl?"

"Seventeen."

Interesting.

When I was eighteen, I'd met a twenty-five-year-old man while bussing tables at a five-star restaurant. He came in a few times, we got to know each other, and then he asked me on a date. I was flattered, and I accepted. At the time, I'd justified our age difference by telling myself I was a lot more mature than most college-age girls. He also looked younger than he was, so I saw no harm in dating him. My mother, on the other hand, was beside herself when she learned of it, and he was shooed away faster than a fox in a henhouse. We never saw each other again, and for a while, I was bitter over my mother's interference. Looking back on it now, I supposed I would have done the same thing if it had been my daughter.

"What can you tell me about the sexual assault accusation made against Grant?" I asked.

"The girl's name is Jenny Conroy. Her father, Rick, was the one who filed charges."

"Were they living in California then?"

"Nope, Las Vegas, Nevada. She still lives there."

"What was the age of consent in Nevada at that time?" I asked.

"It's been sixteen for a while now."

Sixteen, meaning Grant had done nothing illegal.

It was within his rights to pursue Jenny.

"Jenny's father wouldn't have been able to get anywhere if Jenny said it was consensual, right?" I asked.

"Right. Her father tried to argue that Jenny had been seduced by Grant, but it wasn't enough to make the charge stick. Jenny said she consented to the relationship, so nothing more came of it. Until …"

Hunter paused for dramatic effect, and I leaned in closer, eager to hear what else she had to say.

"I think I know why her father made the accusation in the first place," Hunter said.

"Do tell."

"Jenny got pregnant."

"With Grant's baby?"

"I assume so. Jenny listed him as the father on the birth certificate."

Curious, given he'd told me the night before he didn't have kids.

"Why do I get the feeling Grant didn't stick around to parent his child?" I asked.

"Because he didn't. A few months into the pregnancy, he moved to California."

"Where?"

"Los Osos."

Los Osos wasn't far.

Thirty minutes outside Cambria.

"Get this," Hunter said. "By the time Jenny had the baby, Grant was married to someone else, a woman named Kimmie Jenkins."

"How old was she when they got hitched?"

"Eighteen. The marriage lasted just over a year, and then they divorced, citing irreconcilable differences."

I leaned back and crossed my arms, wondering if all of Grant's relationships had been like a revolving door—one woman going out while another one was coming in.

"Did he marry again after Kimmie?" I asked.

"Twice. When he was thirty-one, he married a twenty-one-year-old. They divorced after three years, and two years later, he married for a third time. That marriage also lasted three years and dissolved two years ago."

"Let me guess. The third wife was also a lot younger than Grant."

"Yep, twelve years his junior."

"How old is he?"

"Grant turned forty a couple of months back."

"Rae is right around my age, I'd guess," I said. "Seems odd he'd switch up his pattern of having relationships with younger women for almost two decades to date an older woman now."

Hunter didn't say anything.

She just nodded, causing me to wonder if she was thinking what I was thinking, thoughts I didn't want to believe were true.

Maybe Grant was interested in Rae for all the wrong reasons.

"Does Grant have any other children?" I asked.

"From my research, it's just the one."

I did some quick addition in my head.

"The child would be around eighteen now," I said. "I wonder if he has any involvement in her life."

"Good question."

"Do you have Jenny's contact information?"

"Sure do. It's on my desk. I'll grab it."

"I want you to give it to Simone and ask her to follow up with Jenny. But before you do, is there anything else I should know about Grant?"

"Other than an affinity for relationships with younger women, no. He's super clean. Not even so much as a parking ticket."

Hunter stood and walked to her desk, and my attention turned to the office door and two high-school-age girls who'd just come in. One was tall and slender with long, blond hair. The other was a foot shorter, with a dark, bob-style haircut and a muscular build. Both were dressed like they shopped at the same store in matching crop tops, tennis skirts, and tennis shoes, which seemed ridiculous given the frigid temperature outside.

The girls didn't see me at first, and they made their way over to Hunter.

Blondie said, "We're looking for the detective."

"Which one?" Hunter asked. "There are three of us."

"The one Margot's mother hired."

"When we take a case, we all work together," Hunter said. "So again, which one?"

"The main one, the one who used to be a police detective," Blondie said.

We were all former police detectives, but Hunter, who looked like she'd grown tired of the exchange, knew who they were after. She raised the pen in her hand and pointed me out.

"Take a seat, ladies," I said.

They walked to the chairs across from me and sat down.

"What can I do for you?" I asked.

"I'm Skye Crawford," Blondie said. "And this is Elle Mattox. We're Margot's friends. I mean, we *were* Margot's friends. I mean, we still *are* her friends, but … well, you know what I mean."

Skye leaned back, wiping a tear from her eye, and looked at Elle as if signaling for her to take over.

"We heard about what happened to Margot," Elle said.

"What did you hear?" I asked.

"We know she's dead, and we know she was murdered. She was found in a field outside Cambria, right?"

All information they should not have known yet.

As far as I knew, Foley's press conference hadn't happened yet, so I wasn't keen on divulging more details.

"Where did you get your information?" I asked.

"It doesn't matter," Elle said. "Does it?"

"It might."

"Just tell her," Skye said. "Who cares?"

"Fine," Elle said. "Bronte told her best friend, Kacie, who told Skye, who told me."

So much for Bronte keeping quiet.

"Bronte isn't supposed to be talking to anyone about what we know so far," I said. "We're still trying to figure out what happened. The chief of police will be making a public statement later today."

"Bronte asked Kacie not to tell anyone," Elle said. "And then she told me and told me not to tell anyone, and I told Skye."

It sounded like a typical teenage secret.

Telling one person still made it *seem* like a secret, but one plus one plus one had a way of equaling *everyone*.

"Why are you here?" I asked.

Skye looked at Elle, and Elle said, "There are a couple of suspects we think you should check out."

"Yeah," Skye said. "We *know* things."

I caught a glimpse of Hunter, who was eyeing me like it was taking everything she had not to burst out laughing.

I assumed it wasn't what the girls had said, but how they'd said it, in a high-pitched, know-it-all tone of voice, like they'd cracked the case before we could.

"Let's hear it," I said. "Who do you suspect, and why do you suspect them?"

Elle sat up straight and lifted a finger. "First, there's Isaac Turner. He graduated earlier this year. He's in college now. Anyway, the night of Sebastian's party, we saw him creeping on Margot. He wouldn't leave her alone, even after she told him she was with Sebastian. It's like the guy couldn't take no for an answer."

"It's because he's used to girls falling all over him," Skye said.

"Yeah," Elle replied. "He's used to getting any girl he wants. Well, any girl except Margot. Maybe that's why he had his eye on her. She was a challenge."

"In what way?" I asked.

"Duh, because she was taken. The night of the party, it was like the more she tried to get away from him, the more he kept talking to her, and following her around. I mean, I used to have such a big crush on him, but seeing him fall all over Margot the way he did, it was just—"

"Gross," Skye said. "And pathetic. And stalkery."

I recalled what Sebastian had said about someone letting Kaia into his room the night of the party, staging a scene where Margot would catch them together and make her think a lot more had happened between them than it had. Perhaps Isaac was responsible for the set up … if Sebastian's story was true.

"You said you had a couple of ideas about who may have wanted to do Margot harm," I said. "Who's the second person?"

Skye looked at Elle. "You tell her."

"No, you can."

Skye sat a minute, gnawing at her lip and saying nothing.

"I need one of you to say something," I said.

"Fine," Skye said. "I think Margot was … what I mean to say is, it's probably nothing."

"Define nothing."

The girls exchanged glances again and Elle said, "We were all on the volleyball team together. We weren't even going to try out this year, but Margot said it would be fun, and she was determined for us to all do it together. We liked it, for a while. Then Margot freaked out about the way Coach Warren behaved at one of our away games."

"We didn't see it," Skye said. "He's never been anything but nice to us."

I'd bet he was nice.

Nice didn't mean he hadn't been inappropriate.

"Did Margot say what happened between her and Coach Warren?" I asked.

"He hugged her after we lost the away game," Elle said. "Didn't seem like a big deal to me, but the way she described it, the hug went on a lot longer than it should have. It made her feel weird."

"Did anything else happen between the two of them?"

"A week after the away game, Coach Warren asked Margot if she wanted to keep practicing once we'd finished for the day," Elle said.

"One on one, you mean?"

Both girls nodded.

"And did she?" I asked.

"Once."

"What happened during their private practice?"

"He was helping her improve on her serve."

"Seems like something a coach would do," I said.

I'd made the comment hoping if I feigned innocence, I'd get more information out of them. They liked their coach, that much was clear. It was also clear they were holding back, painting him in a better light than Margot had.

"He's a good coach," Skye said. "He's nice. Everyone likes him."

Almost everyone, it seemed.

"Yeah, but Margot wouldn't lie," Elle said. "She just wouldn't."

"Lie about what?" I asked.

Another pause, and Skye said, "Margot told us Coach Warren was standing behind her during practice, and he pressed his body against hers—like right against it. He was breathing instructions into her ear and stuff. It gave her the creeps."

"Maybe she freaked out over nothing," Elle said. "He could have stood close to her because he was positioning her for the serve. I don't want to get him in trouble if he didn't do anything wrong."

"What happened after Margot shared the information with you two?" I asked.

"She quit the team, mid-season," Skye said.

"We were bummed," Elle said. "She was our best player."

A star player who quit in the middle of the season.

It didn't make sense … unless what Margot had said was true.

"What can you tell me about Coach Warren? Is he single? Married? How old is he?"

"Married," Skye said. "He talks about his wife all the time."

"I'm not sure how old he is," Elle said. "Kinda old. Like thirty?"

If thirty was old, they must have seen me as an ancient relic.

Hunter was still at her desk but hanging on to every word they'd said. She opened her laptop and began typing, looking into Coach Warren, no doubt.

"Aside from the two of you, did Margot tell anyone else what happened between her and the coach?" I asked.

"We don't think so," Skye said. "She was embarrassed."

"What about her mother or her sister? Did she tell them?"

"I doubt it," Skye said. "She said she never wanted us to talk about it again, and we didn't."

They were fidgeting, almost like they were worried it had been a mistake to come to me with this information. If I wanted to keep the connection open, I needed to assure them they could trust me.

"I appreciate the two of you coming to see me today," I said. "I want you to know, anything you say to me will be kept in confidence for now."

Skye smiled, like she was content with what I'd said.

Elle looked worried. "What do you mean, *for now*?"

"When it comes to homicide cases, I work together with the San Luis Obispo Police Department. We have a good relationship, and we try to share information whenever we can. Sharing information doesn't mean I give up my sources, not unless I have to, understand?"

"We do," Elle said.

"I can promise you this—I won't mention your names unless I'm assured they'll be kept in confidence."

"Thank you," Skye said.

They stood, and Elle said, "If someone murdered Margot, they could murder any of us. You need to catch this guy before that happens."

No truer words.

I nodded.

"Rest assured, I'm working on it. Getting closer every day."

And I was. I could feel it in my bones.

18

made a call to Whitlock to fill him in on my day so far. He'd spent most of his morning with Foley, working on what was to be shared with the public during the press conference, which was taking place in a couple of hours. They'd received surveillance footage from the restaurant where Sebastian and Margot were to meet for dinner on the night she disappeared. It would take some time to go through, and I was anxious to know if Sebastian had been there waiting for Margot like he said he'd been.

I told Whitlock I was on my way to see Rae, and by the time I reached her house, he was already there, leaning against his car, waiting for me.

I exited my car, and he walked over to Rae's driveway to meet me.

"How are your blisters today?" I asked.

"Let's put it this way … I'll be keeping my socks and shoes on. Speaking of socks, get a load of these beauties …"

He lifted the leg of his black trousers, showing off the black-and-white leopard-patterned socks he was wearing.

"Nice," I said. "What are you doing here?"

"Foley decided to do the press conference on his own, and I

didn't have anywhere else to be. I thought you might like some company. I know what you're about to tell the good doctor. Why do it alone if we can do it together?"

What hadn't occurred to him was that I preferred doing things like this alone.

I worked better without a bigger audience.

But he didn't know this about me.

I'd first met Whitlock as a child, when he worked as a detective alongside my father and Harvey, my stepdad. I was only a few years old at the time, so I had no memory of him.

Six months earlier, Whitlock came out of retirement to accept the open detective position Foley couldn't get anyone to take. Ever since, Whitlock had made a big effort to be part of my life, which I'd been hesitant about at first. Now, having had the chance to get to know him, I'd grown fond of the guy. I knew the detective position would be filled sooner or later, and I was relieved to know I was working with someone who wanted to work *with* me, not against me. So far there'd been no ego between us, no need to keep things from him about the homicide cases we worked on. Even though he worked for the county, and I worked for myself, there was a level of respect from him that I never thought I'd get as a private investigator.

"I appreciate you for thinking of me," I said. "But I'm all right talking to Rae on my own. We've known each other for a long time."

"Alrighty. Would you like me to leave?"

I felt a bit bad.

I turned toward Rae's house. Through the window, Bronte was eyeing us, no doubt wondering why we were standing in her driveway, having an in-depth conversation. It was then I realized the benefit of Whitlock staying. With his witticisms and engaging personality, I believed he'd provide the perfect distraction.

"If you wouldn't mind sticking around for a while, there is something you could do for me, if you don't mind," I said.

Whitlock clapped his hands together and smiled. "I'm game. Name it."

I bent my head toward the window.

He looked at Bronte and then at me.

"Would you mind keeping Bronte company while I talk to Rae?" I asked. "There are a few things I'd like to go over with her in private. I'd rather Bronte not overhear. Some things are best coming from her mother, not from me."

"Sure thing. Easy-peasy."

"You say that now, but have you spent any time with her?"

"A little." He swished a hand through the air. "I'm not worried. I have three granddaughters. I speak *disgruntled teen*, and I speak it well. All I need is to find an *in*."

"An *in*?"

"A way to connect. I have a few ideas. Let's go."

Before I could say anything more, he'd stepped up to the door and rapped on it. Bronte answered in true Bronte fashion, complete with loose-fitting black attire from head to toe and her signature scowl.

Whitlock stuck his hand out to her. "We meet again! I'm Detective Whitlock, but you can call me Amos."

Bronte looked at his hand but didn't take it. "Uh, yeah. I know who you are."

"Wonderful," he said. "What a fine day it is today. Wouldn't you agree?"

Bronte looked past him at me as if to say, *Is this guy for real?*

They were off to a shaky start.

But at least they were off.

We entered the house, and I leaned toward Bronte, whispering, "How's your mom doing today?"

She shrugged. "Same as every day this week. Quiet. Distant. Emotional."

"Have you heard from Grant?"

"He hasn't been back to the house since he left last night. He talked to my mom this morning. Not sure what was said."

"Hey, Bronte," Whitlock said. "Whadd'ya say we take a walk down to Pattie's Parlour at the end of the street? I hear they make the best ice cream sundaes in town."

"What do I look like … a child?" Bronte asked.

Whitlock lifted a finger. "You can be one hundred and five and still enjoy ice cream."

"I, uhh … I think I'll stay," Bronte said.

"Too bad," Whitlock said. "They also have a dart board. I haven't thrown darts in some time, but I've never been beaten. Don't expect I ever will be, either."

"That's because you haven't played *me*," she said.

"Words are just that, young lady … *words*. Care to prove it?"

"Twenty bucks says I beat you on the first game."

Whitlock tugged at his chin, considering the offer. "I suppose I shouldn't accept such a wager while I'm on duty. But I came out of retirement for this job. Let's live a little, shall we?"

Bronte nodded and then excused herself to pop up to her room and grab a hoodie.

Whitlock turned toward me, a big grin on his face. "See, told you I speak *disgruntled teenager*."

19

A tearful Rae blew into a tissue, her head shaking from side to side after the discussion we'd just had about Margot's homicide and what I knew so far. The night before, it had been hard to admit Margot was dead. Sharing the details about Margot's murder was even harder.

"I can't believe it," Rae said. "Who would do such a thing?"

"Someone who doesn't deserve to live," I replied.

"Are the police sure about what happened? I mean, are they really, *really* sure?"

"As sure as they can be. Silas is thorough. I've never known him to be wrong when it comes to cases like this one."

Rae turned away, her eyes focusing on a photo of Margot sitting on top of a curio cabinet. "She was so good, such a good person."

"I know."

Rae pushed herself to a standing position. "I just ... I need a minute, okay?"

She left the room, and I sat there, the gut-wrenching feeling in my stomach mounting as I thought about what she was going through right now. No matter what I did or what I said, it wouldn't be enough. Nothing would alleviate her pain.

I found myself in an uncomfortable predicament. There were so many questions I wanted to ask her about Grant and Coach Warren. I was desperate to ask them, desperate to solve Margot's case. But speaking to Rae about possible suspects while everything was so fresh didn't seem right.

I couldn't do it to her, not after the news I'd just delivered.

Fifteen minutes passed, then twenty, and I considered writing her a quick note and making my exit. On the one hand, I wanted to be there in her time of need. On the other, I wondered if she was hoping I'd leave.

As I contemplated my options, Rae returned to the living room with two glasses of water. She handed one to me, then sat down. She took a sip of hers and crossed one leg over the other. Looking me in the eye, she said, "So, what happens now?"

"Now you tell me what you need from me and what I can do for you."

Rae's face turned from one of sadness to anger. "You can start by telling me if you have any suspects in my daughter's case."

Rae might have believed that me telling her who my suspects were was a good idea.

Once I did, however, I wasn't sure she'd feel the same way.

"Perhaps now isn't the best time to discuss potential suspects," I said. "You're already dealing with so much. Maybe you need time to process it all. I don't want to make things heavier for you than they already are."

Rae shook her head. "I can't rest until my daughter's killer is behind bars. I want to look him in the eye. I want him to know what it feels like for a mother to lose her child, even though he'll never, ever understand the pain he's caused."

"You deserve that and more."

"If anyone can bring him to justice, it's you, Georgiana. So please, spare my feelings for now. You can't make me feel worse than I already do. I can cry all day, and I do, but that's not going to solve anything."

I drank the entire glass of water she'd given me and set it down, contemplating where I wanted to begin. I hesitated for longer than she'd expected, and she leaned forward, squeezing my hand. "Don't hold back, Georgiana. Whatever you need to say, let it out. I need to hear it. Think of it this way … if I was someone else, someone you didn't know, someone you weren't friends with, you'd say the things you need to say, no matter how hard, wouldn't you?"

I supposed I would.

"I'll stop you if it becomes too much," she added. "I promise."

"You're one of the strongest people I've ever met," I said.

"It's funny you say that. I don't feel strong. Not right now. I'm barely sleeping, and when I do, I have nightmares about … everything, and I didn't even know then what I know now. What if this happens to someone else? It … it just can't. We must stop it. Whether I feel strong or not."

"I think about that too."

She blinked at me but said nothing.

The time had come for me to spill the tea about my short list of suspects.

I decided to start out easy.

"Do you remember the party Sebastian had at his house when his parents were away for the weekend?" I asked.

"Of course. That party was the reason Margot and Sebastian broke up."

"Earlier today, I learned a few more details about that night."

"What kind of details?"

"Margot believed Sebastian had fooled around with the new girl, Kaia Benson. I'm not so sure he did."

"What makes you think otherwise?"

"There's speculation Sebastian was set up to make it look like something happened between him and Kaia. Maybe it did. Maybe it didn't. I have more digging around to do before I know for sure."

"I don't understand. Why would anyone go to the trouble?"

"Do you know a young man named Isaac Turner?" I asked. "He graduated last year."

"I can't say I know him well. His mother is a patient of mine. Why?"

"He attended Sebastian's party, and he may be the reason Margot caught Sebastian in his room with Kaia. Isaac may have orchestrated the whole thing."

"What motive would Isaac have to pull such a ridiculous prank?"

"I hear he liked Margot. During the party, he was following her around the house, flirting with her. She showed no interest, but he was seen pursuing her all night. If what I've been told is accurate, Isaac got shot down and decided to play dirty by finding a different way to get her attention. If Isaac could break Margot and Sebastian up, he could swoop in, be a shoulder for her to lean on—a shoulder with specific intentions."

"Even if what you say is true, it happened a while ago, and Margot has never mentioned anything about Isaac to me."

Not to Rae.

But could she have mentioned Isaac to Bronte?

"I'm guessing here … but if Isaac pulled that stunt to have Margot all to himself and it didn't work, he may have been sitting on a bruised ego since then," I said. "I won't know more until I talk to him and get a feel for what he's like."

"Who else do you suspect?"

"The next two I need to talk to you about will hit a lot closer to home," I said.

Rae stood.

She reached for her glass and held her hand out for mine.

I gave it to her.

"Will I need a cocktail to get through it?" she asked.

"Couldn't hurt."

"Care for one?"

"I'd appreciate another glass of water."

Rae went to the kitchen. A few minutes later, she returned with two more glasses of water.

"What can you tell me about Coach Warren?" I asked.

As Rae sat back down, she jerked her head back like the question had surprised her. "Why are you asking about him?"

The hard part of the conversation had commenced, and it was about to get even harder.

"I heard there were a couple of instances where Coach Warren made Margot feel uncomfortable," I said.

Rae raised a brow. "Are you serious? In what way?"

"He hugged her once after they lost a game, and Margot felt the hug went on for too long. He also had a one-on-one session with her to help her improve her serve. According to Margot's friends, he had his body up against hers. It creeped her out, so to speak."

"I know about the private session, but I don't know any of the details from that day. What I don't know is … where are you getting this information?"

From behind us, I heard, "Yeah, I was just about to ask the same question. Whoever is telling you this stuff about Coach Warren is a liar."

I turned.

Bronte's eyes bored into mine like a bull ready to charge.

Whitlock stood behind her, looking apologetic for not keeping her away longer.

"I can't discuss how I came by the information yet," I said. "I also want to add, I haven't spoken to Coach Warren to get his side of the story."

"Here's a thought … maybe you should talk to him first before you slander his name, accusing him of something he didn't do," Bronte spat out.

There were so many things on the tip of my tongue to say in response, none of which was appropriate to utter in this moment—or any other—so I stayed quiet.

"Coach Warren also teaches math," Bronte said. "I've taken his class. He's a good guy. He's not a pervert."

"I'm just telling your mother what I've been told," I said. "And just so you know, I haven't spoken to anyone else about what I've heard."

Yet.

"Give up your source," Bronte demanded. "Who's saying this stuff?"

"I can't discuss it right now."

"Then you shouldn't be talking about him at all, should you?" Bronte said.

It struck me as odd that she was so invested in Coach Warren's innocence just like Margot's friends seemed to be.

"Coach Warren has never said anything he shouldn't have or done anything he shouldn't have," Bronte said. "If you think someone as nice as him is a suspect, you must not be very good at your job."

"Bronte Grace Remington!" Rae said. "That's enough."

Bronte tossed her hands in the air. "What? I'm just being honest."

I rose from my chair, intending to step outside for a moment before I could no longer contain my words, and Whitlock sidled up next to me.

He faced Bronte and said, "Georgiana is an excellent detective. If she suspects someone, she has good reason. I'm sure it's not easy to trust her, or to trust me. But believe me when I say, we are doing everything we can to solve this case."

"Whatever," Bronte said. "I'm outta here."

She grabbed a set of keys off a metal key holder on the wall and took off for the front door. Rae called after her, but a second later, the door slammed, and the house went quiet.

Whitlock glanced at each of us in turn and said, "I was just about to head out, but maybe I should stay."

"I'm all right," I said. "There are a few more things I need to discuss with Rae."

"I'll leave you to it, then," he said. "You ladies have a good night."

He gave us a two-finger salute and disappeared down the hallway.

Rae looked distraught, like she'd had just about as much as she could handle, and I wasn't even finished yet. She'd need a lot more than a glass of water to get through the next part.

20

There's one more person I need to talk to you about," I said, returning to my seat.

"Based on the way you're looking at me, you saved the worst for last," Rae said. "Who is it?"

"It's Grant," I said.

Rae blew out a long sigh and said, "If you're wondering whether we've spoken today, we have. Twice."

"Has he asked to come over?"

"Yes and no. He's still shaken up over what happened last night with Bronte. I get the feeling he doesn't want to see her just yet."

I crossed one leg over the other. "How are you feeling about it all?"

"With everything going on, it's hard to know what I feel about anything. I'm numb, and I don't have the capacity to invest in our relationship right now. It's unfair to Grant, I know, but I need to take some time for myself, and for Bronte. This morning, I looked in the mirror and I wondered how long it will take before I regain some semblance of the life I had before all this happened. I feel like I never will. I tried telling all of this to Grant, and I had been sure he'd heard me and understood … until he tried to tell me all the reasons I need him by my side right now."

"It doesn't sound like you want him here," I said.

"I don't. It has nothing to do with him, or me not wanting to be with him. He doesn't get it. He's never been a parent, never experienced this kind of loss."

Except he *was* a parent.

An absent one.

I took a deep breath in and said, "What do you know about Grant's past?"

"He's talked about it. Are you asking about any specific event in particular?"

"I am. Are you aware of his past relationships?"

"He's spoken to me about his exes. Why?"

"He's been married multiple times."

"I'm aware."

"He has a history of having relationships with women who are a lot younger, starting with a woman he pursued when she was seventeen and he was twenty-two."

"Jenny Conroy. Her father tried to split them up. Grant told me all about it."

"Jenny had a child," I said. "She listed Grant as the father on the birth certificate."

She rubbed her forehead and sighed. "And you're wondering why he hasn't seen her for all these years?"

"I am. I'm also curious about why he was so quick to marry another woman before Jenny even had the baby."

Rae took a few gulps of water and set the glass down. "There's a simple explanation. Jenny's father threatened to disown Jenny if she didn't break things off with Grant. Her father was adamant Grant have no part in the baby's life. Grant said he's made several attempts to see the child over the years. Jenny has always refused him."

"If he's the father, he has rights. He could have taken it to court."

"Oh, he's the father, all right. Angela looks just like him. And you're right. Grant could have fought for custody."

"So why didn't he?" I asked.

"Jenny called him once and put Angela on the phone. I believe he said she was around seven years old at the time. Angela stayed on the phone just long enough to tell Grant she hated him."

"Did she say why?"

Rae nodded. "Jenny had told Angela that Grant had abandoned them when she became pregnant because he didn't want a child. During the call, Angela told Grant she had a new daddy, one who was much better than him."

Harsh, and if true, a despicable thing for a mother to do to her child.

"Angela would be eighteen now," I said.

"They haven't spoken since the phone call all those years ago, but thanks to social media, Grant keeps up with Angela and what she's been doing. Six months ago, Grant learned Jenny's father died. With him gone, I believe it's time for him to make an effort to be in Angela's life again."

"Do you think he will?"

"I do. We've had several conversations about it."

Rae stretched her arms out to the side and yawned.

"I can go, if you're tired," I said.

"It wouldn't matter if you did. I don't sleep much anymore. Have you finished talking about Grant, or is there more?"

There was more.

Plenty more.

"As Grant has aged, he has continued dating women much younger than himself."

"What are you getting at?"

"As far as I know, you're the only older woman he's dated. I guess I'm trying to figure out what made him change his pattern."

"After Grant's most recent divorce, he realized there were things about himself that he wanted to work on. He's been seeing a therapist for about eight months. He's immersed himself in it, which I find impressive. I believe it's changed his life."

I was starting to see another side of Grant, a side that made me question whether I'd been wrong to think he could have been involved in Margot's murder. Then again, Rae hadn't even been with Grant for six months. Everything was still fresh and new, and I suspected her rose-colored glasses had yet to come off. She was close to him, perhaps too close to see what she didn't want to see—the fog instead of the clearing behind it.

"Why do I get the feeling Grant's failed marriages are not the reason you wanted to talk about him?" Rae asked.

"They're part of the reason."

"You consider him a suspect, don't you?"

"Among others we've discussed."

"What has he done to make you think him capable of harming my daughter, let alone killing her?"

Nothing.

Aside from a tiff with Bronte, he'd done nothing.

And if I was being honest with myself, the fact Bronte wasn't too keen on him shouldn't have sounded the alarm. She had issues with most people.

"You're right," I said. "It's easy for me to suspect those closest to the family. I question anyone and everyone. It doesn't mean they're guilty."

Grant would remain on my suspect list for now. Even with Rae's attempt to paint him as a decent person, I couldn't rule him out.

"Aside from Grant, Isaac, and Coach Warren, is there anyone else you suspect?" Rae asked.

"I'm still considering Sebastian."

"Why?"

"He seems genuine in the affection he felt for your daughter, but he keeps popping up here and there in my investigation. He said he was at a restaurant, waiting for Margot the night she disappeared. This morning I learned the police have acquired the surveillance footage from the restaurant. It will either give him an alibi or poke holes in his story."

Rae leaned back and crossed her arms. "Sebastian's been in my home many times. He's a good kid, and he comes from a good family. I believe he's telling the truth."

She'd shot down half of my suspect list, but there was one man she hadn't stood up for yet.

"Bronte is so sure Coach Warren isn't involved," I said. "Based on what you know about him, would you agree?"

"I would like to believe he's a good man. But after hearing your version, I started thinking about Margot's behavior around the time she'd quit the volleyball team."

"What can you tell me about it?"

"It was unlike Margot to quit anything. She always stuck things out, even when it was difficult. I was shocked when she said she didn't want to be on the team anymore."

"Did she give you a reason?" I asked.

"She didn't, and I questioned her several times, in fact. I even talked to Coach Warren about it."

"What did he say?"

She paused a moment, as if trying to recall their conversation. "He asked if I knew why she was quitting. I said I didn't. Then he asked if I would try to talk her into remaining on the team, which I did. It didn't work. A few days later, I spoke to him again. He asked me to pass along a message to Margot."

"What was the message?"

"He wanted her to stop by after class and speak to him."

"And did she?"

"She told me she'd met with him, that they talked, and she'd said her mind was made up. I felt I'd pushed it enough at that point. I'm not one of those parents who forces their children to stay involved in a sport or activity if they don't enjoy it. It was *her* life. All I ever wanted was for her to be happy."

"You're a good mother, Rae."

She raised a brow. "Am I? When it comes to Margot, I feel like I missed something, something that may have kept her alive. I'll spend the rest of my life having to live with the fact that I'm still here and she isn't."

"There's nothing you could have done, trust me."

"Does it ever go away—the pain, the remorse, the what-ifs? Does it ever get better? You've been through it. I need to know."

I rose from my chair, walked over to Rae, and wrapped my arms around her. "It doesn't go away, but it *does* get better, if you let it."

As the tears began to fall, she said between sniffles, "I've been doing a lot of thinking this week. What I need more than anything right now is family. Several years ago, I did something I'm not proud of, and I never realized just how much it would impact my life until now."

I leaned back and looked her in the eye. "Do you want to talk about it?"

"It's silly, to be honest, a stupid fight I had with my brother, Jay. We haven't spoken much since. I doubt he even knows what's happened with Margot."

"Stupid fights can be resolved. I've resolved more than I care to admit."

"After all these years, I'm not even sure he'll talk to me. Ever since Margot went missing, I haven't been able to stop thinking about him and how much I wish he was with me right now. Our parents are both dead. He's all the family I have left."

"Do you have his phone number?" I asked.

She nodded. "As long as he hasn't changed it."

"It seems now is the right time for me to go. *You* have a call to make."

21

I exited Rae's house and found Whitlock and Bronte sitting on the porch, side by side, laughing.

"I can't believe you were a speed skater," Bronte said. "And I can't believe you almost went to the Olympics."

"What can I say," he said. "I'm a man of intrigue."

"You might be the sickest old guy I know."

"Is 'sickest' a good thing?"

"It's like … cool. You're cool."

"Gee, thanks." He turned, looking up at me. "How's Rae doing?"

"She's all right," I said. "She's going to call her brother. They haven't spoken in a long time."

"*You* convinced my mom to call Uncle Jay?" Bronte asked. "I'm impressed."

"I wouldn't say I convinced her. I'd say she realizes she might need him in her life right now."

"Huh. I can't even remember the last time I saw him. I was a kid."

Whitlock brushed a hand down his trousers like he was dusting off lint and then stood. "This sick old guy needs to get going. It was nice spending time with you today, Bronte."

"Yeah, it wasn't as bad as I thought it would be."

We said our goodbyes, and I watched the man I'd forevermore refer to as the 'Teenager Whisperer' get inside his car. As I watched him drive down the road, I noticed someone sitting inside of a silver pickup truck several houses down.

Nothing nefarious about that, right?

Still, I wondered why anyone was idling there.

I made a mental note of the time, and Bronte smacked a hand against the concrete, looking up at me as she said, "Wanna sit down?"

I sat, shocked she'd offered me an invitation.

"I … uhh … you know, I feel a little bad about before, about what I said to you in the house," she said.

Feeling a *little* bad wasn't *a lot* bad, but it was something.

"You're going through a lot right now," I said. "I get it."

"Yeah, I'm not always a … you know, a—"

"It's all right. You don't need to say it. I'm not always one either. Sometimes though …"

She smiled like she appreciated me going easy on her.

"The detective told me some things about you," she said.

"Good things, I hope,"

"Most of it was good."

"Are you saying some of it wasn't?"

"I'm saying some of it was depressing and sad."

It explained why she was being so nice.

"We all have our hardships in life," I said. "I believe it's the reason why some of us connect with one person more than another."

She ran a hand through her hair and said, "Can I ask you a question?"

"Sure."

"Do you think Coach Warren hit on my sister?"

"I don't know yet. You seemed convinced it didn't happen."

"I mean, I know what I said before. I've had some time to think about it."

"And how do you feel now?" I asked.

"Confused. I still think he's a good guy. He's always been good to me, anyway."

It felt like there was something more, something she wasn't saying.

Maybe she needed a gentle push.

"You think he's a good guy, *but* …?"

"Margot didn't lie. If she did, there would have to be a dang good reason for it. That's why I want to know who talked to you about Coach Warren."

I crossed my arms, thinking about the promise I'd made to Elle and Skye.

"It's not that I don't want to tell you," I said. "I made a promise to keep their identities a secret, for now. I'm trying to honor their wishes. Besides, you know what they say … snitches get stitches."

Bronte burst out laughing.

"You're funny," she said, "for a weirdo."

"I like to think weirdos make life more interesting," I said.

"From one weirdo to another, we do. And I get it. You're not going to tell me who talked to you. Fine. You said 'their wishes,' which means, it wasn't just one person. It was at least two."

"I did."

"I bet they're on the volleyball team, aren't they?"

"I can neither confirm nor deny."

Bronte went quiet, and then she said, "Tell me this … do you believe what they said about Coach Warren?"

"When they came to me, it was obvious they were nervous to share information, which made them seem credible. I wouldn't be surprised to learn there's some truth to their story. I also believe they like Coach Warren, and they only came to me because of Margot's disappearance."

Bronte bent her knees and wrapped her arms around them. "Let's say the rumors about Coach Warren are true. Why wouldn't Margot come to me about what happened? We were close, but now, I don't know what to think. She was keeping things from me, and I don't understand why."

"People keep things to themselves for a lot of reasons. Sometimes it's because they feel like by keeping quiet, they're protecting those around them."

Bronte shook her head. "Margot never needed to protect me. If anything, it was the other way around."

"I know it's hard to accept that she had secrets, but most of us do."

I'd said the words in the easiest way I knew how, hoping I wouldn't offend her. I never knew when something I said would set her off. It looked like she was about to respond, but she went silent again.

"We can stop talking if it's too hard or too much or too … whatever," I said.

"I need to … umm, show you … Hold on a second."

She pulled a note out of her pocket and handed it to me. "The day after Margot went missing, I found this note. It's in her handwriting."

"Where?"

"Over the visor in my car. I pulled it down, and it fell into my lap."

"Why would someone leave a note above your visor?"

"It's where I keep my sunglasses."

"Have you shown the note to anyone?" I asked.

"Just you. Right now."

I opened the note.

It was short but telling.

Bronte,

There's something I've been meaning to tell you, a secret I haven't shared with anyone. I get why you're mad about me seeing Sebastian, but I have my reasons. I didn't just end things with him months ago because of what happened at his house party. There's another reason, one I've needed time to work through. I haven't wanted to talk about it until now, and I really need your advice.

When you're ready to talk, let me know.

"What if Coach Warren was what she hadn't told everyone about?" Bronte asked. "What if *he's* what she needed time to work through? I still don't want to believe it, but it kinda makes sense."

If Margot was referring to Coach Warren in her note, she had confided in Elle and Skye, which would have meant she *had* told someone … unless there was more to it, more about Coach Warren that Margot hadn't said.

I folded the note and looked at Bronte.

"Thank you for sharing this with me," I said. "I'd like to keep it for a while if it's all right. Chief Foley and Detective Whitlock will want to see it, and they should."

Bronte shrugged. "Yeah, I guess. I've been trying to decide whether to tell my mom about it. She's going through so much already."

"I think she deserves to know."

"Fine, I'll talk to her."

"I have a question for you," I said. "What do you think of Grant?"

She huffed a snarky laugh. "Do you mean this week, or in general?"

"In general."

"I don't know. I guess I've never given him a chance."

"Why not?"

"He's not right for my mom."

"Why not?"

"She likes time to think about the decisions she makes, even small ones. Ever since they started dating, I feel like he's been pushing her to make decisions before she's ready."

I didn't know Grant well, but I could see what she was saying. There was an undercurrent about him of impatience and unease.

"Can you give me an example?" I asked.

"A couple weeks ago, I overheard Grant tell my mom they should move in together. They haven't even been dating that long yet."

"How did your mother respond?"

"She told him she wanted to think about it and that it was

something she'd need to talk to us about first. He didn't get why our opinion was necessary. He said the decision should be between the two of them. He also said if my mother felt the same way about him that he felt about her, there was nothing to think about."

Pushy *and* manipulative.

"Sounds like Grant was trying to guilt your mother into doing what he wanted without factoring in her concerns or needs."

"Yep."

"I understand your behavior toward him now, and the reason why you're so protective of your mother."

I shifted my attention to the truck I'd seen on the street. It was still there. Except now I could see there were two people inside the cab, not one.

I checked the time.

Fifteen minutes had passed.

"Hey, ahh … thanks for being here for my mom," Bronte said. "She thinks a lot of you."

"I'm here for you too, if you want me to be."

She snorted a laugh.

"Too much?" I asked.

She grinned and said, "A little. I should check in on my mom."

I had no problem wrapping things up. Then I could get a closer look at the pickup and who was inside it.

"One last question," I said. "The night of Sebastian's party, one of the guys was flirting with Margot."

"Yeah, Isaac."

"You know about him?"

"Yeah, Margot told me he followed her around like a wounded puppy. At first she didn't mind, but it bothered her when he wouldn't leave her alone. The guy couldn't take a hint."

"What can you tell me about Isaac?"

Bronte considered the question. "He's a moron, and he's full of himself. Why?"

Blunt and to the point.

I liked it.

"Would you say he's the type of person who has to have his way?" I asked.

"Oh, yeah. For sure."

"There's a chance Isaac set up Sebastian and Kaia to make it look like something happened between them that night when it hadn't."

She stared at me for a moment and said, "Are you being serious?"

"I am."

"I was so angry when I heard about what happened that night. I never even questioned whether the story was true or not. I should have. When I confronted Sebastian at school the week after the party, he was gutted. At first I told myself it was just an act to get me out of his face. Now ..."

"You and Sebastian are talking again. Has he said anything?"

"He told me he talked to Kaia. They don't think anything happened between them. He tried telling me all this a while ago, but I was too furious back then to listen. Last night, I did, and I felt like crap after I'd heard what he had to say. He's had my back so many times in the past. I should have heard him out back then, and I didn't."

"You are now, and that's what matters."

She reached into her pocket, pulled out a piece of gum, and unwrapped it, popping it into her mouth. "Yeah, well, I just hope he's telling the truth. What if Margot's secret was about Isaac? What if he's the one who killed her? I'm going to find out."

Margot's secret could have been about Coach Warren, or Isaac, or Sebastian, or anyone else for that matter.

"Let me question Isaac," I said.

"When?"

"As soon as I can. Please don't confront him or Coach Warren until I do."

"I mean, I'll *try*. I want answers. I'm not just going to sit here and wait for … *hello*? Are you even listening? What are you looking at?"

The truck.

"Sorry, I got distracted," I said.

"By what?"

I pointed at the truck. "Do you see the pickup parked in front of the blue house?"

Bronte leaned forward and looked past me, squinting as she stared in the direction I was pointing. "What in the hell are they doing here?"

"Who are you talking about?"

"Do they think we need a babysitter? We don't."

"I'm not sure what you mean," I said. "Who's trying to babysit you?"

Bronte gritted her teeth and bolted off the porch, speed-walking in the direction of the pickup.

I took off after her.

As we neared the vehicle, I confirmed there were two males inside, one of whom I recognized. The guy in the driver's seat took one look at Bronte and threw the truck into reverse. In his effort to get away, he backed over one of the neighbor's mailboxes, and then he slammed on the brakes, jolting the truck to a stop.

22

Bronte yanked open the passenger-side door of the truck and laid into both guys, ending her rant with, "What are you two idiots even doing here, anyway?"

Sebastian, who refused to make eye contact, said, "I … uhh, I watched the, you know, the chief of police's press thing today, and I messaged Danny. He said we should head over to your place and make sure you guys were all right."

Danny leaned forward, raising a hand as he looked at me and said, "Hey."

He was a bit on the scruffy side. He had long, auburn hair that fell past his shoulders, numerous tattoos, and a black hoop nose ring. His overall look screamed "tough guy," but he had kind eyes, eyes full of genuine concern.

"Hey," I said.

"I'm Danny."

"Daniel Moffat? Bronte's boyfriend?"

"Yeah."

"If you two are here to check on Bronte and her mother, why are you parked over here?" I asked. "Were you trying to be sneaky?

If you were, you did a lousy job. I've had my eye on you for a half an hour now."

Danny smacked Sebastian in the shoulder and said, "See? I told you she saw us."

Sebastian said nothing.

"I still don't get *why* you're both here," Bronte said.

"A killer is out there," Danny said.

"Yeah, we're aware," Bronte said. "So?"

"What if he's not done … you know, killing people? What if he plans on targeting you or your mother next? Someone needs to be here to look after you."

"We're fine," Bronte said. "Thanks for checking. You guys can go now."

"No way," Danny said. "I don't care if you want me here or not. We're here, and we're not leaving. Deal with it."

Based on the expression on Bronte's face, I thought she might reach across Sebastian and slug Danny in the face. Instead, she walked to the driver's-side door and opened it. She jumped onto Danny's lap, and they kissed for more Mississippis than I cared to count.

"That might be the sexiest thing you've ever said to me," Bronte said.

Sebastian and I exchanged glances, and he got out of the truck.

I looked at him and said, "Why don't we go for a walk?"

I guessed spending time with me was the last thing he wanted to do, but as the lovefest between Bronte and Danny continued, he agreed.

"I want to show you something," I said.

I pulled the note Bronte had given me out of my pocket, opened it, and handed it to him, pausing a moment while he read it.

When he finished, I said, "Let's walk, and we can talk about the note."

He nodded, and we headed toward Rae's house.

"It's Margot's handwriting," he said.

"Bronte found it above the visor in her car the other day. I believe Margot wrote it a couple of hours before she was abducted."

"I don't get it. I thought we broke up because of what happened at the party."

"Looks like there was another reason. Do you have any idea what she was talking about in her note?"

He shook his head. "I don't think it's about me."

I disagreed.

I believed it had something to do with him, and I couldn't decide whether he was feigning innocence or he *was* innocent.

"I never suggested the note was about you," I said. "When you were dating, was there anything going on in her life that gave you concern?"

"Nothing. She was happy."

"What about after you broke up?"

"She didn't want anything to do with me, so it's not like I'd know if something was going on with her after we broke up."

"There are a few people I still need to question. I'm hoping when I do, I'll have some answers, or at least more clarification on the meaning of her note. One of those people is Isaac Turner. Did you invite him to your party?"

"I did. We were on the football team together. A bunch of us hung out this summer, and he showed up a couple of times. I saw him talk to Margot a time or two, but I didn't think much of it. I trusted her, and I figured I could trust him. Never took him for the type of person who'd go after another guy's girl."

"When did you find out Isaac was interested in Margot?"

"Right after the party. My friends saw him following her around that night. Guess he even tried to kiss her."

"Did you confront Isaac about it?"

"I saw him a few weeks after we broke up. He said something about it not being his fault that I couldn't keep my girl, and I decked him."

Sebastian decked him, which told me he had issues controlling his anger. Then again, so did I when the situation warranted it.

"Why didn't you tell me about this before now?" I asked.

"Look, I'm all over the place. I'm doing the best I can. When I thought I had a shot at winning Margot back a week ago, I started picturing what our lives could be like in the future. I just wanted to be with her. I didn't care about anything else. Sounds stupid, right?"

"What's stupid about it?"

"You probably think I'm too young to know what I want in life."

"I wasn't. I was thinking about the man I'm with now and how I felt about him when we first met. I was in college. Back then I pictured life with him in the same way you did with Margot. He pictured life with me too, but neither of us admitted it. We didn't see each other again for over twenty years. A few years ago, we reconnected. We've been together ever since."

"Wow."

"I'm sorry your second chance was taken from you," I said.

We came to a stop on Rae's driveway, and Sebastian turned toward the house. He stared at it for a long time and then said, "I have so many memories here."

His breathing quickened, and he wiped his eyes, turning away from me as he tried to control his emotions. For a moment it seemed like he'd calmed himself down, and then he bent over, resting his hands on his knees as he said, "I can't stop thinking about what she must have gone through that night. I bet she was scared. Scared and alone. I'd give anything to turn back time and stop it from happening."

I grabbed a tissue from inside my bag and handed it to him.

He wiped his eyes and his nose. "Sorry."

"There is no need to apologize," I said. "You've been carrying a heavy weight. It's good to let it out."

As his breathing steadied, he said, "Are you going to talk to anyone besides Isaac?"

I wanted to tell him about Coach Warren, if for no other reason than to see the look on his face when I did. People's expressions had a way of giving even more information than words did sometimes.

"I'm going to speak with Coach Warren," I said.

Sebastian screwed up his face, confused. He, too, seemed unaware of Margot's feelings toward the coach or the reason why she'd quit the volleyball team.

"Why do you want to talk to the coach?" he asked.

Given he appeared to have no knowledge of Coach Warren's alleged behavior toward Margot, I decided not to say much.

"The coach spent a lot of time with Margot and the other girls on the team this year," I said. "Maybe he knows something we don't. Is there anyone else you think I should talk to at school?"

"I can't think of anyone."

"I imagine the press conference was hard to watch," I said.

"It would have been a whole lot easier if my mom hadn't come into my room while it was on. She'd been watching it in the living room, and she started crying and decided we should talk about it. When I told her I didn't want to, she got on a Zoom call with her friends. They were all crying and talking about what they should do … like there was anything they *could* do, and I just wanted to get out of there."

"I know you're trying to be strong for yourself and everyone around you, Sebastian, but it's okay to allow yourself time to process what's happening," I said.

"Every day I wake up thinking things can't get any worse, and then they do. I've been worried about Bronte and Rae, and I just wanted to be here."

I turned and saw Danny driving toward Rae's house. Bronte was next to him, snuggled up against his arm. He pulled to a stop in the driveway, and they both got out.

Danny looked at Sebastian and said, "We should order some pizza."

"Sounds good to me."

Danny slung his arm around Bronte and said, "You think your mom would be okay with us hanging out tonight?"

"If she's not, I'm sure we can talk her into it." Bronte turned toward me. "You can stay."

"Thanks, but I have somewhere else to be."

And that somewhere was an unannounced visit with a young man named Isaac Turner.

23

I figured Isaac was staying at his mother's house for the holidays. Hunter gave me her address, and as I drove over, I realized I'd been so wrapped up in Margot's case, I'd almost forgotten Christmas was a couple of days away.

I parked and made my way to the door, which was adorned with one of the biggest flocked wreaths I'd ever seen. The wreath was covered in blue lights, which blinked off and on every few seconds.

I knocked on the door and was greeted by a woman I presumed to be Isaac's mother. She was petite and had long, white, braided hair which fell over one of her shoulders. She was a lot older than I expected, given Isaac had just graduated high school.

"Hello," I said. "Are you Isaac's mother?"

She nodded. "I'm Donna."

"I'm—"

"There's no need, dear. I know who you are. You run that private eye business over on Main Street."

In a town with a population under six thousand, I shouldn't have been surprised.

"Is your son at home?" I asked.

"No, he's not right now," she said. "Why do you want to speak with him?"

It was a question I'd expected, and one I wasn't ready to answer, not with full disclosure. "I'm trying to piece together the last few months of Margot's life. I was hoping your son could help."

"Did he know her?"

"I believe he did," I said. "I'm sure he's heard about what happened. I imagine just about everyone has by now."

Donna tapped a bare foot to the tile floor. "We were talking earlier about what the chief of police said on television this afternoon. Well, *I* was talking about what the chief said, at any rate. Isaac was in a hurry to get out the door and meet up with a few friends. He grunted something about how sad the situation was, and that's all he had to say on the matter."

"Do you expect him home soon?"

"Oh, yes. He texted me a half an hour ago, saying he'd be on his way home soon. Would you like to come in? I'm sure he'd be happy to help with your investigation if he can."

Once he knew what questions I had for him, I was sure he wouldn't.

But that was a problem for later.

I followed Donna to the living room, which had been decorated with one specific theme in mind—it was a shrine of Isaac. I guessed there were at least fifty photographs of him, all in white frames, ranging in age from baby pictures to what I assumed he looked like now. Photos were everywhere—on the walls, the coffee table, the hutch, and even a couple of end tables.

I walked around the room, taking my time as I moved from one photo to the next. In Isaac's most recent photos, I found him to be tall, muscular, and attractive, with short, black hair and sparkly, topaz-colored eyes.

"Your son's a good-looking guy," I said.

"He's my miracle child. I wasn't sure I'd ever have kids before he came along. I was married for about twenty years to a fellow named Harold. He was nice man, a good man, but he made it clear he never wanted children. I convinced myself he'd come around to the idea one day, so I froze my eggs. It was a brand-new procedure at the time. Wasn't even sure it would work."

"Did Harold know you froze your eggs?"

She shook her head. "Not until after we divorced. By then, I couldn't imagine living the rest of my life alone. So, I found a surrogate, and about a year later, Isaac was born."

"Did you remarry after the divorce?"

"Heavens no. One marriage was enough for me. I had no desire to become involved with another man after our split. Harold and I have managed to remain friends all these years, if you can believe it. He comes to my place for dinner twice a week, and he's done so since the day he moved out."

"Harold may not have wanted children, but I imagine he was a father figure to Isaac if he was around so often."

She nodded. "I was surprised how fast Harold took to Isaac. It was instantaneous, the first time he laid eyes on him. A few months later, he even suggested we get back together and make another go of it. But I liked the way we were apart a lot more than when we were together. It was more spontaneous, I suppose. More of a friendship. Less expectations and less … oh, let's see now, what's a good word … *stale*. Yes, that will do."

There was something to be said for a person who spoke their truth. And I'd always believed that just because something worked for one person didn't mean it worked for another. Donna seemed like a woman who knew herself, knew what she wanted, and went after it. Not everyone could say that about themselves, though I couldn't help but wonder whether she leaned on her "miracle child" a little too much at times.

How would she feel one day when he married?

Would she be able to handle another woman coming into his life, a woman who took time away from her?

As I contemplated those questions, Donna turned toward me and said, "Are you married, dear?"

"I'm engaged."

"When's the wedding?"

"We haven't set a date yet."

"Good for you. I've always thought it best not to rush these things."

Try telling that to my mother.

The front door opened, and Isaac came strolling in, eyeing me like he wondered who I was and what I was doing there.

He was about to find out.

"Son, this is Georgiana Germaine," she said, "the detective everyone in town is talking about. She stopped by to speak with you about Margot Remington, the young woman who died."

His face went white, and he turned, removing the backpack from his shoulder and sliding it onto a hook on the wall. He cleared his throat and approached me.

"Why do you want to talk to me about Margot?" he asked.

"I want to discuss your relationship with her," I said.

"We didn't have a relationship."

"You ran in the same circles, attended the same parties … you know, like the one at Sebastian Chandler's house not too long ago."

I smiled at him.

It was the kind of smile that let him know I *knew* things, lots of things.

He frowned and looked at his mother. "Hey, Mom, can I talk to the detective alone real quick?"

"I don't understand why I can't be here while the two of you talk," she said.

"The detective's right. I knew Margot. I haven't talked about her before because … given our history, it's something I don't like talking about. Might be easier for me to do if we were alone. Don't worry. I'll fill you in on everything later."

Smooth.

Don't think for a second I won't tell your mother what I know if I have to … because I will.

Donna was reluctant, but she nodded, adding, "Before Georgiana arrived, I was going to have a bath. I suppose I can do that now."

"Thanks, Mom," Isaac said.

She said goodnight and left the room.

Once her bedroom door closed, Isaac looked at me and said, "We can talk, but not here."

24

saac wanted us to chat in private, something I assumed he'd suggested so his mother wouldn't overhear the conversation. Or had he suggested it for a different reason—one I hadn't figured out yet?

I walked behind him, descending the stairs until we reached the basement. We stepped inside, and Isaac closed the basement door behind him and leaned against it.

He tipped his head to the side and said, "I'm guessing you've heard some things about me, or you wouldn't be here."

"What is it you think I've heard?" I asked.

"Depends on who you've been talking to, I guess."

"I've talked to a lot of people this week. I've met with some of your former classmates, Margot's family, and a handful of others. Right now, I'm just gathering information."

"I'm not sure I have anything useful to say."

I didn't believe it.

I took my cell phone out of my handbag. He looked at it, and his eyes widened.

"What are you doing?" he asked. "You can't record me."

"I'm not recording you. I'd need your consent."

"What are you doing then?"

"Taking notes," I said.

He walked over to a beanbag chair and plopped down on top of it. I remained standing.

"I didn't have anything to do with what happened to Margot," he said.

"I never said you did."

"I didn't even know her. Not much, anyway."

"Well, that's not true, is it? You liked her, didn't you?"

"Yeah, so what?"

"Didn't anyone ever tell you it's not cool to hit on the girlfriend of one of your friends?"

"I wouldn't call Sebastian a friend. We played football together, hung out a handful of times. That's it."

"How did you meet Margot?" I asked.

"She started working at a coffee shop last year. I used to stop by there every day after school. They had a protein shake I liked to get before my workouts."

"Was Margot single when you first met?" I asked.

"She told me she was, and the way I saw it, I showed interest in her first, which means I had first dibs."

What an odd comment.

"You can't stake a claim on a woman just because she's single. Women aren't pieces of property, Isaac."

"I didn't mean it like … look, all I'm saying is that from the first day we met, there was a vibe between us. She felt it too."

"How did you know? Did she ever say she had feelings for you?"

"It's one of those things you just know. I'm never wrong about these things. Besides, women are drawn to me. Some say it's the hair, but I say it's my dimples. Flash a smile, and they can't resist. Works every time."

I almost coughed out the word *narcissist*, but I didn't.

"Tell me about the conversations you two had at the coffee shop," I said.

"We didn't always get the chance to talk. Depended on how many customers were there and who was working. When it was just us, we talked about all kinds of things. The more I got to know her, the more I started to see she wasn't like other girls."

"How was she different?"

"She was deep … in conversation, I mean. I could talk to her about any subject, and she could keep up. It impressed and surprised me."

"Why?"

"I started to feel something for her, which was weird. I've never gone for her type in the past."

"And what *type* would that be?"

He tapped a thumb on the beanbag, thinking. "Cute nerd, I guess."

Isaac was doing a great job of digging his own hole so far.

I didn't even need to provide him with a shovel.

"Did Margot know you started to have feelings for her?" I asked.

"I'm sure she did."

"Did you *tell her* you liked her?"

"Not in so many words. We flirted here and there. I assumed she knew."

He *assumed* she knew.

Assumptions like that were dangerous.

"How did you behave toward Margot when you saw her outside the coffee shop?" I asked. "I assume you ran into each other at school this year before you graduated."

"She was a couple grades below me, so we weren't in any of the same classes."

"I doubt there are even two hundred students in the entire high school. Seems to me like you would have seen her just about every day."

He didn't seem to know what to say to my comment, and he went quiet.

I waited.

"Yeah, so maybe I didn't talk much to her outside of the coffee shop," he said. "I don't think it bothered her. She never said anything about it."

"Why didn't you talk to her when you saw her at school? It seems to me like you were trying to keep the fact you were interested in her a secret."

"Why are you giving me the third-degree here? She's dead. What does me talking to Margot or not talking to her have anything to do with your investigation? None of it matters."

It mattered because I was trying to establish a timeline for Isaac and Margot, starting from the day they met. If he didn't speak to her at school, it told me he didn't want people to know he was interested in her. At some point before Sebastian's party, that changed.

But when?

And why?

"When did you learn Margot was dating Sebastian?" I asked.

"Must have been a couple of months after she started working at the coffee shop. I went in after school one day, and she was more excited than usual. I asked her about it, and she started telling me about Sebastian. She thought I'd be happy for her. When I wasn't, she was shocked."

"Do you think she was shocked because you brushed her off at school, and you never made her aware of your feelings?"

"When she started rambling on about Sebastian, I straight-up told her I liked her … because it made me mad. She should have talked to me before she got with him, and I told her so."

"How did Margot respond?" I asked.

"She tried to say she thought we were just friends. There's no way that was true. She knew I liked her. She just refused to admit it."

It was easy for Isaac to point fingers, knowing Margot wasn't around to defend herself.

"How did the conversation end?" I asked.

"I stopped going to the coffee shop. We avoided each other at school. Then I graduated, and I didn't see her for a couple of months, not until the night I was invited to the party at Sebastian's house."

The night everything changed.

"You knew Margot was dating Sebastian," I said. "So you knew she'd be there."

"I did. Figured it wouldn't be a big deal, but when I walked in and saw them together, all the memories we'd shared at the coffee shop came rushing back. She belonged with me, not him."

"You were seen spending time with Margot at the party."

"Yeah, we talked. She acted weird, almost like she didn't want to be seen with me, which made no sense."

"Maybe she acted the way she did because she wasn't used to you talking to her outside the coffee shop."

"Who knows?"

"What can you tell me about the party?" I asked.

"It was just like every other party. I hung out with friends, stayed until the party was over, and I left."

It sounded innocent enough, if not for the fact he'd left out one crucial part of the evening's events.

"Sebastian and Margot broke up the night of the party," I said.

"I heard."

"You were the one who caused the split."

He leaned back and grinned. "I'm not sure who you've been talking to, but you don't have your facts straight."

"Cut the crap, Isaac. I know what you did. You set Sebastian and Kaia up to look like they'd been inappropriate with each other when they hadn't even come close. This, in turn, played a role in Margot and Sebastian's breakup."

I noticed a glint of mischief in his eyes.

"I mean ... I may have orchestrated a *little something* so Margot could see Sebastian wasn't the right guy for her," he said.

"It wasn't about him being the right guy or the wrong guy. It was about her picking him over you. What did you think—they'd break up, and she'd run to you for comfort?"

He grinned even wider. "What can I say? They broke up. My plan worked, didn't it?"

He acted like it was a personal achievement, like he'd done nothing wrong by meddling in someone else's relationship. But how had he felt when he *didn't* get what he wanted? He broke them up, but he didn't get the girl.

How angry had it made him?

Angry enough to commit murder?"

"Let's go back to the start of the party when you arrived and tried to talk to Margot," I said. "What did you say to her?"

"I explained why I hadn't talked to her since the day she told me about Sebastian. And yeah, she was still mad about how I'd reacted, which told me she cared about me, even if she spent most of the night telling me to leave her alone."

"Moving on to Sebastian and Kaia being found in his bedroom together. You sent Kaia to his room that night."

He turned his palms up. "What can I say? I saw an opportunity, and I took it. Maybe he shouldn't have been so drunk."

"What you did was low and classless. It speaks to the kind of person you are."

Isaac jerked his head back, stunned.

At first I thought he'd have some clever retort. Instead, he said, "Wow, you think you know me. You don't. You don't know a thing."

The more we talked, the more it became clear that he had spent his entire life believing he was entitled. Sure, his mother doted on him, but perhaps a little too much. He seemed to have the idea that he could do anything he wanted to anyone he wanted as long as it served his purpose.

He didn't hide from it, either.

He bragged about it, speaking without regret.

"Did you see Margot again after the party?" I asked.

He nodded. "The next day. I waited in the parking lot for her to get off work. When she walked out, I told her I heard about what happened with Sebastian, and I let her know I was there for her if she wanted to talk or whatever."

"And did she?"

"Not at first. Then we got into my car and chatted for a couple of hours. I felt closer to her than I ever had."

"You must have believed you had a chance with her after your conversation."

"With Sebastian out of the way, I figured I did. I told her I still had feelings for her."

"What did she say?" I asked.

"Not what I wanted to hear, that's for sure. She said she needed time to think about what I'd said. A day went by, then two, and then more. I never heard from her again."

His plan to lure Margot away from Sebastian hadn't worked.

I wondered how often he had thought of her since he'd left for college, and if he'd seen her since he'd returned home for the holidays … on the night she went missing, perhaps?

"When Margot didn't get in touch with you, how did it make you feel?" I asked.

Isaac snorted a laugh. "What, are you my shrink now?"

"Have you ever seen a shrink?"

"I did. Once. I didn't get anything out of it, so I stopped going."

"Why did you start seeing a therapist in the first place?"

He cocked his head to the side. "Wouldn't you like to know."

"When did you get back into town?"

"A couple of weeks ago. Before that, I was here for Thanksgiving. Stayed through the weekend before heading back to school."

"Did you see Margot either of those times?"

"Once. I was having lunch with a friend in town. She walked in to pick up some food she'd ordered."

"Did you talk to her?"

"Nope. She waved, and I acted like I didn't see her."

He glanced to the side and went quiet, like he was thinking back on it.

"I shouldn't have acted the way I did," he said. "How was I supposed to know it was the last time we'd see each other?"

"When was that?"

"Don't remember."

"This visit or your last visit?"

"Last visit."

"Margot went missing on Monday," I said. "Where were you that night?"

"Here, with my mom. I wasn't feeling well. Flu or something. Didn't leave the house for a few days."

From the moment I'd stepped foot in the basement, I'd noticed an object that stood out among all the rest in the room. I was drawn to it—its color, its shape, what it was made from.

It looked … *familiar*.

Clarity found its way to me at the start of our conversation, and I'd sent a text message when I'd told Isaac I was taking notes—a text message that was about to pay off.

As the doorbell sounded upstairs, Isaac's eyes narrowed.

"Who could that be?" he asked. "We didn't invite anyone over."

"You didn't. I did."

"Why?"

I lifted a finger, pointing at the object sitting on one of the shelves of a bookcase. "Where did you get that?"

He turned, staring at the object in question.

"None of your business," he said.

"Except it *is* my business, because it sure as hell looks to me like a piece of brown wicker—wicker I believe is a piece of the basket from Margot's Beach Cruiser."

The basement door opened, and I turned. Donna walked in, followed by Whitlock. She rubbed her eyes, blinking a few times like the unexpected visitor had roused her from sleep.

"The detective says he's here to ask you a few questions, Isaac," she said.

"You need to quit letting everyone in the house, Mom," Isaac said. "You know you don't have to, right? They're not allowed inside unless they have a warrant."

Speaking of warrants ... I looked at Whitlock and said, "Did you get it?"

He pulled a folded piece of paper from his pocket and said, "I sure did."

Whitlock handed the warrant to Donna.

"Whatever it says, I can't read it," she said. "Not without my glasses."

"Give it to me, Mother," Isaac said.

She handed it to him, adding, "I'm sure it's nothing. We haven't anything to hide. Best we cooperate, don't you think?"

Donna may have had nothing to hide.

But I doubted the same could be said about Isaac.

"Will you please explain why you have come here with a search warrant?" Donna asked. "Search warrants are only served to people who have done something wrong, right? I can assure you, we have not. This must be some sort of misunderstanding."

"We have reason to believe your son is in possession of a piece of the wicker basket off Margot's bike," Whitlock said.

"A piece of wicker?" Donna asked. "It makes no sense. Why would my son—"

"Good question," I said.

I walked over to the piece of wicker and pointed at it, noticing a small sticker affixed to it, a sticker that read: *Life is too short to wait.*

"Where did you get this, Isaac?" I asked.

He sighed in frustration. "You want the truth? I forgot all about it. And it's not what you think. I mean, okay, maybe it *is* what you think, but not for the reason you're thinking it. I wouldn't have suggested talking in the basement if I knew you'd go berserk and ask your detective friend here to get a warrant."

"How did it get here?" I asked.

With all eyes on Isaac, it didn't take long before he felt pressured into giving us an answer.

"All right, fine," Isaac said. "When I heard Margot was missing, I got curious, and I decided to check out where her bike was found. I wanted answers, same as you. I wanted to know what happened and why it happened. I found a piece of her basket in the weeds … and yeah, I took it."

"Why did you take it?" I asked. "Because so far, it doesn't make any sense."

"That sticker … I gave it to her. I knew she collected them. Her stuff was always covered in stickers."

"When were you at the crime scene?" I asked.

"I dunno. Maybe a couple of days after she went missing."

"When you weren't feeling well, you mean?" I said. "Earlier tonight you told me you were sick when Margot went missing. You said you didn't leave the house for a few days."

"I didn't leave … except the one time."

"You lied," I said.

"Yeah, I guess I did. You were asking a lot of questions."

I wondered what else he was lying about.

During our conversation, I'd been studying Donna's reaction to what was being said. It seemed to me she was doing everything she could to refrain from making facial expressions of any kind. But her eyes gave her away, expressing how she felt in this moment—shocked.

Was she in shock because her son had lied and he hadn't been home when he said he had? Or was it because he had a piece of a murdered woman's bicycle basket in his possession? Or both? Donna had been under the impression her son didn't know Margot well. I expected she was questioning everything he was saying at this point … just like we were.

Whitlock studied Isaac for a moment and said, "Let me make sure I'm hearing this right. You're saying you went to the crime scene a couple of days after we started searching for Margot. While there, you just happened to stumble on a piece of her wicker basket. And not just any piece. A piece containing a sticker you had given her."

Isaac shrugged. "I know how it sounds, but it's the truth."

"Well, that there was a dandy story you just told," Whitlock said. "Problem is, I don't believe a word of it. Here's why. We searched the entire area where Margot's bike was found. Not just once, multiple times. We recovered every piece of her bike except for one—that there piece of wicker. I'd say it's time for you to tell us a different story. How about telling the truth for a change?"

Isaac's hands began to tremble.

Donna took a step toward him, a look of worry on her face.

Isaac raised a hand, saying, "No, it's okay, Mom. I'm fine."

He wiped his hands on his pants, and for a moment, we stood in silence.

Then Donna approached her son, taking his hands in hers.

"What's going on, Isaac?" she asked. "I don't understand what's happening right now. You said you didn't know Margot. Not well. And now you're saying you gave her a sticker, and she put it on her bike. I'm so confused."

If Donna believed she was helping his cause, she was not.

But she was doing a swell job of helping ours.

Isaac stared into his mother's eyes and whispered, "I was there."

"You were where?" I asked.

"The night Margot disappeared, my mother wasn't home. She was playing bingo with a few friends at the community center. I was asleep when she left. When I woke up, I was sweating, and I had a fever. I went to the kitchen to see if there was any stronger medication I could take, and I couldn't find anything."

"So you left the house," I said.

"I did. I went to the store to get some medicine. On the way back home, my headlights flashed on what looked like Margot's bike on the side of the road. I recognized it because she used to ride it to work sometimes. I got out, looked around, found the piece of her wicker basket with the sticker I'd given her, and I just took it."

I recalled a conversation I'd had with Foley at the start of the investigation.

"It was you, wasn't it?" I pressed. "You were the one who called the hospital the night Margot went missing. You called to see if she was there."

"Yeah, it was me."

"Why did you call the hospital and not the police?" I asked.

"I didn't think to call the police. I didn't know she'd been abducted. No one did. Her house wasn't far from ours, so I did a drive-by on my way home. All the lights were out. Everything seemed normal, so I just came home. It wasn't until later that I found out she was missing."

Isaac's new story seemed a lot more plausible than the other one he'd told, but given we'd caught him in multiple lies, I wasn't sure what to believe.

Was this new version of his story the truth?

Or was it an even more elaborate lie?

Had he called the hospital on purpose to make it seem like he didn't know where she was ... when she was in fact, with him?

"I need to take you down to the station for questioning," Whitlock said.

"Why?" Isaac asked. "I've told you everything I know, all of it. There's nothing more to say. I've already said I had nothing to do with Margot's disappearance."

"People often think they've talked about everything," Whitlock said. "Nine times out of ten, there's always more. If you're innocent as you claim to be, a few more questions couldn't hurt. Right?"

"My son *is* innocent," Donna said. "He's telling the truth."

The *truth* was ... Donna wasn't home that night.

The *truth* was ... Isaac had no alibi.

Was he as innocent as he professed?

I had my doubts.

I envisioned a scenario in which Isaac returned home for the holidays, saw Margot at the restaurant, and the feelings he had for her came flooding back, just as they had at the party. Feelings that led to frustration over being told *no* when he was used to being told *yes*. Feelings that turned him into a cold-blooded killer.

26

It was the day before Christmas, and given it was also Sunday, Giovanni and I were expected at my mother's place for family dinner. Ever since Margot had gone missing, it felt like the days were bleeding into each other, so much so, I'd lost track of them. It was like I'd rowed my boat into the heart of the ocean and was uncertain how to find my way back. I wanted clarity, and I wanted it now, and it didn't feel like it was within my reach.

As a result, I wasn't in much of a celebratory mood, and though I'd spent the morning toying with ideas on how to bow out of tonight's family dinner, it wouldn't change anything. I'd be going whether I wanted to or not. My mother wouldn't have it any other way, and I had no intention of disappointing her. When it came to the holidays, nothing meant more to her than being together with family.

My phone buzzed on the nightstand, and I reached over and picked it up, hoping I had a message from Whitlock or Foley. Before I'd left Donna's house the night before, I'd filled Whitlock in on everything Isaac had said before he'd arrived. I'd heard nothing since Isaac was taken in for questioning, and I was anxious to know what was going on.

The message I'd received was from Hunter, giving me a home address for Coach Warren. I slipped on a twenties-era silk robe and walked to the kitchen. Giovanni was standing in front of the oven, whistling to an Italian tune playing through the new speakers we'd just had installed. He slid a hot pad over one hand and bent down, cracking the oven door open.

Peering inside, he said, "The quiche I made is just about finished. Another fifteen minutes and you would have been served breakfast in bed."

I grinned and shot him a wink. "I can get back in bed if you prefer."

"I *prefer* to have you here with me."

"Then I'll stay." I slid onto a barstool, squeezing my eyes open and closed a few times. "I went to bed at a decent hour last night, but I feel like I haven't slept in days."

"That's one mystery I can help you solve. You talked in your sleep off and on throughout the night."

"Oh, no. I'm sorry."

"Don't be sorry. It can't be helped."

"I hope I didn't keep you up."

"You were fine."

"Do you happen to remember what I said?" I asked.

"Some of it. You mentioned Margot several times. You said you knew who was responsible for her death."

"I did?"

"You did."

"Huh," I said.

"Do you know who's responsible?"

"I don't. Not for certain."

"Are you getting any closer to figuring it out?"

"If anything, it feels like I'm getting further away from it," I said. "Did I talk about anything other than Margot?"

Giovanni leaned against the counter, crossing one leg in front of the other. "It was hard to make out, *cara mia*. You were mumbling at times, and your sentences were jumbled together. Most of what I could make out were names. You brought up Coach Warren and Rae's boyfriend, Grant. Someone named Isaac. Oh, and you also mentioned Sebastian."

It made sense.

All of them had consumed my thoughts over the last week.

"Each time I interview a suspect, I think they're going to slip up, say something to me to let me know they're the killer," I said. "I'm closer to solving the case but not close enough."

Giovanni pulled the quiche out of the oven and set it on the stovetop to cool. "Is there anyone you haven't interviewed yet?"

"Margot's volleyball coach. She quit the team before the season was over and told a couple of her friends the coach had been inappropriate with her."

"In what way?"

"Little things like pressing his body against hers. He also hugged her after they lost a game for what she considered to be too long."

"Sounds like a prime suspect to me. When do you expect to speak with him?"

I wasn't sure he'd like my answer.

"Hunter texted me his address this morning," I said. "I'd like to stop by and talk to him *if* you can spare me. I know we always spend Sunday together, but would you mind if I did a little investigating for the first part of the day?"

"You're working a case right now. I'm aware it's your priority, as it should be."

Except he was my priority too, and I struggled with the idea that I'd been absent more than he deserved of late.

"Want to meet for lunch?" I asked.

"Sure, what time?"

"One o'clock at the Boathouse Diner?"

"I'll be there. I assume you're still planning on dinner at your mother's house?"

I shot him a wink. "Unless you have any idea how I can get out of it."

"I haven't the slightest idea, nor would I suggest one. Not when it comes to your mother."

It was a safe answer, and one I'd expected. Even Giovanni knew it was far easier to give in to my mother's wishes than to go against them.

He grabbed a couple of plates from the cupboard, placed a few strips of bacon on each, and tore another couple of strips into pieces, sprinkling them over Luka's dog bowl. Luka, who had been lounging by the door, keeping an eye on us as we chatted, perked right up. In seconds he'd scampered over to his dog bowl, inhaling the contents in their entirety in seconds.

"How big of a slice of quiche would you like, my dear?" he asked.

"I think half of the pie should do it."

He laughed and sliced a modest piece, sliding it onto a plate next to the bacon. He handed the plate to me, along with some silverware and a glass of orange juice. He dished up his own plate and joined me at the bar.

As soon as he set his plate down, he wrapped his arms around me from behind, giving me a nice long embrace.

"You'll get through this case," he said. "You always do. But first, you need a decent breakfast. You haven't eaten much all week, and I promised your …"

He let the words he hadn't said trail off, but I knew what he'd stopped himself from saying. He'd promised my mother he'd make sure I was eating. She knew better than anyone how often my appetite fell by the wayside when I was working a case like the one I was now.

"It's all right," I said. "I know my mother calls you when she can't get through to me."

"If I can keep her happy and you fed, I'm doing my job. Speaking of jobs, let's eat. The sooner I get you out of here, the sooner I get you back."

In theory, I hoped he was right.

But something told me today wasn't going to go as planned.

27

I stepped up to Coach Warren's doorstep and pressed the doorbell. A petite, sweet-looking woman with big brown eyes, a bob haircut, and a wide smile opened the door. The first thing I noticed was how she was dressed—in a tank top and short shorts. Given it was winter and the current temperature was in the mid-fifties, I wondered how she managed to wear so little and keep warm. As soon as I stepped into the house I had my answer when I was blasted by a surge of hot air blowing out from the heater vent.

I managed to introduce myself and tell her about the case I was investigating before the hot flashes began. I stripped off my jacket, and she took it from me, hanging it on a wooden coatrack in the foyer.

"I'm Cass, by the way," she said. "Warren is in the shower. He's been in there for a while now. He likes his long steam showers in the morning. Why don't you head on into the living room, and I'll let him know you're here."

"I appreciate it, thank you."

Cass pointed in the direction of the living room. Then she turned, making her way down a short hallway into the back bedroom.

The house was on the smaller side, and the boxy layout reminded me more of a condominium than a house. What it lacked in size was made up for in its tasteful décor. The house was decorated in a coastal theme, with shades of blue, white, gray, and tan. Everything matched. On the wall above the sofa was a four-panel painting on canvas of a giant blue whale. On a shelf I spotted a series of small glass bottles, all lined up next to each other. Inside the bottles were shells, and on the outside, the bottles had been labeled with the city where I assumed the shells had been collected.

A photo album rested on the coffee table in front of the sofa. I glanced over my shoulder, and when it appeared there was no one in sight, I ventured a peek inside. The album was filled with places Warren and Cass had visited together over the years. I saw no photos of children. But not everyone had children nowadays.

"We've been adding to that album for more than ten years now," a male voice said. "We take turns choosing the destination and travel somewhere different for a couple of weeks every summer."

I snapped the album closed and faced him.

At first glance, the coach wasn't what I expected. He was short and lean and reminded me of a squeaky-clean, boy-next-door type.

He crossed his arms and said, "I've been wondering when you'd stop by. Some of the kids at school reached out to me and said Dr. Rae hired your agency to investigate Margot's ... well, I guess it's a homicide now, isn't it? What a shameful, horrible thing. And to such a sweet young woman. My wife and I were devastated when we heard the news."

Devastated, indeed.

The expression on his face seemed sincere enough.

The comment he'd made about how he'd been waiting for me to stop by was not only frank, it struck me as odd.

Why would he assume I'd stop by at all?

It was a question worth asking, so I did.

"I wasn't aware you expected me to pay you a visit," I said.

"Given I was Margot's coach, why wouldn't you? You're questioning everyone who knew her, right? That's what I've been told."

He made no attempt to hide the fact he'd had his ear to the ground. It was almost like he wanted me to know he was keeping up with what was happening on the case.

"You're right," I said. "I am questioning everyone."

He sat down on the sofa and gestured for me to sit in the chair opposite him, which I did.

"Ask me anything you like," he said. "I'm an open book."

He may have perceived himself as an open book now, but would he feel the same way when he learned the true nature of my visit?

"You coached Margot in volleyball at the start of the year, but she didn't stay on the team for the entire season," I said.

"No, she did not."

"Why not?"

"You know, I've wondered the same thing myself. It was like one day everything was fine, and the next, she started acting like a different person."

"Different in what way?"

"Hard to say. I always assumed we had a good relationship. We'd talk here and there, as I do with all the young ladies on the team, and we seemed to get on well. One day, it all changed. I'm not sure what happened. She shut down, started acting distant. She even canceled one of our sessions."

"When you say *sessions*, do you mean private sessions, or sessions with some of the other young women on the team?"

"Most of the time, I don't offer private sessions."

Most of the time.

Not *all* of the time.

"Why not?" I asked.

"Ever since this whole 'Me Too' movement, I'm always concerned about whether I'm saying or doing the right thing. You can't be too cautious nowadays. At the same time, I suppose I want them to think of me as a friend. I do everything I can to be the kind of coach they can look up to—someone they can count on. High school's tough. These kids are dealing with all kinds of hardships these days."

"Did you ever have a private session with Margot?"

"Once. I made an exception, and I made sure to let her mother know in advance that it would be a one-on-one session after school. Dr. Rae signed off on it."

"Why did you make an exception for Margot?"

Cass entered the room and took a seat beside her husband, sitting so close to him, she was almost on his lap. She took his hand and smiled at me, saying, "What are y'all talking about?"

My first instinct was to ask her if she would mind if I continued the conversation with him without her being present. She seemed like a Chatty Cathy, and I worried she was the kind of person who'd intervene at every turn. Right now, I needed him to remain focused. But she'd welcomed me into their home, and so far, he was answering my questions. To suggest she leave the room didn't seem appropriate, and I just hoped her being glued next to him wouldn't change things.

Warren looked at his wife and said, "The detective is asking me about the one-on-one volleyball session I had with Margot."

Cass swished a hand through the air. "Oh, that. Why would you be askin' about that?"

Because your husband might be a predator.

"I'm asking everyone about their relationship with her," I said. "I'm trying to learn as much as I can about Margot's life in the months before she died."

"To answer your question, I made an exception for Margot because she wasn't like any of her other teammates," he said. "I don't mean to put down on the other young ladies on the team, but Margot was by far one of the most driven athletes I've ever known."

"In what way?"

"She had one goal, and that was to win. She stayed behind a lot after practice, long after everyone else had gone home, so she could work on things that needed improving. She was a natural. I couldn't believe it when she told me she'd never played before. I'm certain she could have gotten a scholarship if she would have stuck it out and hadn't … you know …"

"*Died*," I said.

As soon as I said it, they went silent.

Cass used a finger to blot a few tears from her eyes and said, "I know, I'm a big softie. I didn't even have a personal relationship with her, but to think about what the dear heart must have gone through when she died. I can't imagine. We, ahh … we heard the funeral is in a couple of days."

"Are you planning on attending?" I asked.

Warren nodded. "We feel it's important to pay our respects to Margot's family."

"Yeah, we want to go to show our support," Cass added.

About that …

"I need to tell you both something," I said. "What I mean to say is that I need to warn you."

Warren raised a brow. "Warn us about what?"

I'd been pacing myself, working my way up to the heavier questions, the questions he might not want to answer. Now I was faced with a rather unpleasant situation. I needed to explain why they might not be welcome at the funeral and find a way to ask the hard questions *and* have them answered.

There was no delicate way to go about it, not that I had ever managed to be delicate in situations like these, even if I tried.

"There's no easy way to say this, so I'm just going to say it," I said. "A couple of people came to see me at my office yesterday, people who knew Margot. They wanted to talk to me about something Margot had confided to them before she died."

"You're looking at me like whatever they confided is related to me in some way," Warren said.

"There were a couple of times during the volleyball season when Margot felt you were inappropriate toward her, Warren."

"What do you mean?" he asked. "What did she think I did wrong?"

"I promise I'll get to it. Before I do, it's important you know that Margot's sister, Bronte, has been made aware of the allegations. If you know her at all, you know she's feisty, and at times, she has a temper. If she sees you at the funeral, I'm not sure how she will react."

Cass looked at him, and they both looked at me, stunned by what I'd just said. And the blows were about to keep on coming.

Warren stood and began pacing, running a hand along his jawline as he said, "I'm sorry … you were told what, and by whom?"

"A couple of individuals came to me in confidence. I'm unable to reveal their identities to you, but I will tell you what was said. I'm not here to accuse you of anything. I'm here to tell you what they told me and to get your side of the story."

"I understand," he said. "Please tell me. Tell me everything."

28

'd expected Warren to get defensive as soon as I mentioned allegations had been made against him. He surprised me when he sat back down on the sofa, took his wife's hand, and squeezed it tight. The chipper man who'd greeted me after I arrived now looked lost and forlorn, like the air had been sucked right out of him. Cass didn't look much better.

As I sat there, thinking about how to explain what I'd been told, I had a distinct feeling. Nothing about this man screamed *murderer*.

Not. One. Single. Thing.

It didn't mean he wasn't one.

"I'd like to talk to you about one of the away games this year," I said. "A game the team lost … right before Margot quit."

"I believe I know the one you're referencing," he said. "I can still picture the look on Margot's face when the game ended. It was a look I'll never forget. We were tied. The opposing team served, and the ball came to Margot. She went to spike it, and as she jumped up, she winced, like she'd injured herself. Instead of doing one of her classic spikes, the ball went into the net. It was game point, and we lost."

"It sounds like Margot blamed herself for the loss."

"She did. Out of curiosity, why mention that game in particular?"

I took a deep breath in and said, "Do you remember what happened after the game?"

"Sure, I do. Margot was angry, furious at herself. She said she let her team down, and there was nothing anyone could say or do to convince her otherwise."

"Did you speak to her about it?" I asked.

"I tried. It's like I said before when I mentioned I'd noticed a change in her behavior. The young woman I knew her to be didn't seem to have an angry bone in her body. Sure, she was hard on herself at times, and she expected a lot of herself, but even then, she was kindhearted. The night she blamed herself for the loss, she acted different, almost like she was someone else. It was a side of her I had never seen before."

"Do you recall the date of that away game?"

Cass piped up, saying, "It would have been right around Labor Day. I remember because we went to a barbecue at a friend's house. Dr. Rae was there, and Warren spoke to her about Margot's unusual behavior."

"What was Rae's reaction to what you told her?"

"She was aware the team lost, but she didn't know the details about what happened," Warren said. "Margot hadn't said a word about it. Dr. Rae said she'd talk to her, but I'm not sure if she did."

Labor Day would have fallen right after Sebastian's party in August. Perhaps the breakup was to blame for the abrupt change in Margot's behavior. It seemed plausible she would have been reeling over it. Whether she was or not, it didn't change the fact that I was at Warren's home to ask him a couple of uncomfortable questions, the first of which was teed up and ready to go.

"Do you remember hugging Margot the night of the away game?" I asked.

"I sure do. Is this one of the complaints that was brought to your attention?"

I nodded.

"I can explain," he said.

"Please do."

"After the game, I tried everything I could think of to get Margot to calm down. When she didn't, I just … well, I threw my arms around her and hugged her. It was a gut instinct, and I acted on it. I never looked at it in terms of appropriate or inappropriate. I was trying to be supportive of how she was feeling in that moment."

"Margot thought the hug went on for too long," I said.

He looked at me and shrugged. "I don't recall how long it lasted. Maybe she was right. Maybe it did, but it wasn't intentional. It's like I just said. I was a coach, trying to comfort a member of my team. There was nothing more to it. I swear."

"Since when is it a crime to comfort another person?" Cass added.

"If we're living in an age where I can't do something as small as that and not have it turn into a problem, I'm not sure I want to coach anymore," Warren said.

He seemed sincere, and I found myself wanting to believe him. Hugging a student had turned into somewhat of a gray area, an area that had changed a lot since I was in high school. In the gray, it was hard to see whether something like a hug was or wasn't okay. All I had to go on were the words a young woman had shared with two of her closest friends. Words that, if true, meant that whether the hug given by Coach Warren was innocent or not, the fact remained that it made her uncomfortable.

A hug was a far cry, however, from raping a young woman and burying her in a shallow grave just outside of town. If Warren was guilty, I needed to prove how a hug had escalated to the point of murder, and why, which led me to question two.

"Let's talk about the one-on-one session you had with Margot," I said. "When did it take place?"

Warren gave the question some thought. "A couple of weeks after we lost the away game."

"I was told you suggested the two of you have a private practice."

He looked shocked.

"I have never offered to meet with my students alone," he said. "I've already told you that I cleared it with Dr. Rae first. Ask her, she'll tell you. I would also add that we weren't alone during our practice session. There were students and members of the faculty coming in and out of the gym the entire time. Ask Barbie Leonard, the physical education teacher. She was around that afternoon."

I jotted her name down and said, "Thanks, I will."

"Why are you asking about the one-on-one session I had with Margot?"

"She said you pressed your body against hers during that practice. She also said you whispered instructions into her ear in a way that didn't seem appropriate."

He hung his head and went quiet.

"This is all a big misunderstanding," Cass said. "My husband would never come onto a high school student, or anyone else. He's a loving, devoted man. I have never had a single reason to doubt him."

It was what I expected her to say, Cass standing up for her husband in the same way Donna had stood up for her son.

"I'm just telling you what I heard," I said. "I'm not accusing Warren of anything. I'm just here, trying to have a candid conversation with you both."

"Whether you are accusing him or you aren't, you heard wrong," Cass said. "Plain and simple."

"Now, honey," Warren said, "the detective's just doing her job. She's here trying to get justice for Margot and her family so they can move on. There's no reason to get upset."

"No reason to get upset?" Cass said. "How can you sit here, knowing this gossip is being spread about you by who knows how many people in this town and remain so calm?"

"I don't think it's being spread around," I said.

"How would *you* know?" Cass asked. "All it takes is one rumor, one match to light the fire, and my husband could be out of a job."

Warren patted his wife's hand. "All right, all right. I hear you. I understand your concerns."

"Do you? Because I don't think you do!"

Cass shot up and raced down the hall, slamming the bedroom door behind her.

We exchanged glances, and I said, "If you want to go after her, I understand."

"I appreciate it, and I will in a minute. Before I do, I feel like I should make a few things clear."

"Go right ahead."

"If I had any idea my behavior had made Margot uncomfortable, I would have done everything in my power to make it right. I never want one of my students to suffer over a misunderstanding when I could have cleared it up."

"When Margot quit, didn't you wonder why?" I asked.

"Of course I did. The day she came to my office and told me she no longer wanted to be on the team, I thought she was joking at first. When I realized she wasn't, I asked why she was giving up after she'd come so far in such a short time. She said she didn't want to talk about it, and then she thanked me for everything I'd done for her."

"She *thanked* you?"

"She sure did. Then she turned around and walked out. Thinking back on it now, I suppose I should have gone after her."

"Why didn't you?"

"I was in shock. I sat there not knowing what to do or how to convince her to change her mind. In the end, I wanted her to stay on the team, but I also wanted to respect her wishes."

If Warren's story was true, I had to wonder why Margot thanked a teacher she'd told her fellow classmates had been inappropriate with her. Something about it didn't fit. Had she thanked him because she felt awkward in his presence and wasn't sure what to say so she overcompensated by giving him a false compliment? The notion seemed too easy. I couldn't shake the feeling I was missing an important connection—one I hadn't made yet.

For now, it would have to wait.

There was somewhere else I needed to be.

"I have to get going," I said. "I appreciate the time you took to talk to me today and how open you were to answer my questions."

Warren nodded, stood, and walked me to the door.

"I know you don't know me, but I hope by talking to me today, you were able to get an idea of the kind of person I am," he said.

"I have."

"If you have any other questions, please, stop by again sometime."

"I will."

I stepped onto the front porch, and he said, "Would it be all right to ask you what you think now that you've spoken to me?"

I paused, taking a moment to consider how to put my thoughts into words. "I'll say this for now. I want to believe what you've told me is true."

"It's a start. May I ask you for a favor?"

"What's the favor?"

"If Bronte believes I may have had something to do with Margot's murder, I believe it's best if my wife and I do not to attend the funeral. We'll send flowers to Dr. Rae and let her know we're here for her if she needs anything."

"I believe you're making the right decision," I said. "You still haven't mentioned the favor."

"Would you be willing to speak to Bronte and tell her what we discussed today?"

"I'll speak to her, but Bronte strikes me as the type of person who gets something in her mind and runs with it."

"I'm aware. I've witnessed it firsthand at school. Not toward me, of course, but toward her fellow students."

"If I may, I'd like to offer you a word of advice before I go. If Bronte shows up here, do everyone a favor and don't answer the door."

F oley was inside his truck in front of the San Luis Obispo
Police Department when I pulled up beside him.

He put his window down and said, "I was wondering
when I'd see you today."

"And I was wondering about the conversation you and
Whitlock had with Isaac last night," I said.

"The kid's a real smartass, but as to whether he had anything to
do with Margot's murder, we're not sure. For now, we're keeping an
eye on him. We're also looking into his background to see what
comes up."

"What did he say when you brought him in for questioning?"

"As soon as we started asking questions, he asked to call his
lawyer."

"He has a lawyer?"

Foley nodded. "His college roommate's father."

"Why call a lawyer if he's not guilty of anything?" I asked.

"We've been asking ourselves the same question. Asked him
too, come to think of it."

"What did he say?"

"He believes you're trying to pin Margot's murder on him."

"He's not wrong. I'll pin him to the wall if he's guilty."

"When Isaac first came in, I was trying to get a read on him, but his lawyer arrived before I got the chance. Next thing I know, the lawyer's applying all kinds of pressure. He claimed we had no right bringing Isaac in for questioning. He also accused us of being buddies with the judge who signed off on the search warrant, which is complete crap, of course. Everything we do is by the book."

It made sense now why neither Foley nor Whitlock had followed up with me. They'd been shut down at the start. There wasn't much to say about their time with Isaac.

"I'm guessing he was released almost as soon as he arrived," I said.

"Yep. It was late, and I was tired, and I didn't have it in me to go a bunch of rounds with his lawyer. I have no problem hauling Isaac back in here, but before I do, I'll make sure I'm prepared for anything his lawyer throws at me."

"I'm glad I got the chance to talk to Isaac before the lawyer got involved," I said.

"You've spent more time with Isaac than we have. What's your take on him?"

"Seemed guilty to me, but maybe it's because I wanted him to be. He lied to me, he lied to Whitlock. And his story about taking a piece of the basket off Margot's bike is just weird."

"Higgins and Decker searched the place," he said. "They didn't find anything."

"Out of everyone I've talked to so far, Isaac strikes me as the type of person who could be capable of murder," I said. "It's not just his demeanor. It's a look he gets in his eyes. I'm not sure how to explain it except to say it's like he has a screw loose."

"I know the one. Saw it myself. That's why we're doing our due diligence, retracing his steps from the time he arrived home for the holidays to now."

"I can have Hunter look into his background more too."

Foley tapped a thumb to the steering wheel. "I should warn you. Isaac's lawyer is no joke."

"Noted. Thanks for the heads-up."

"If you see him again, don't provoke him. The kid must have brought you up at least a half a dozen times while we were questioning him. It's almost like he has some weird obsession with you."

"And here I was thinking we were on the road to being best friends," I said. "Bummer."

I laughed.

Foley did not.

He wagged a finger in the air, saying, "I mean it, Georgiana. I know how you are sometimes. Might be best to steer clear of the kid. Not forever, but for now."

"Okay. I got it."

"What's on your agenda for the rest of the day?"

"I'm working this morning, but promised Giovanni that I'd take the rest of the day off."

"Not a bad idea. I think we could all use a break. Who knows? Maybe it will help us see things from a different perspective."

"Before I go, I wanted you to know I spoke to Coach Warren this morning."

"I heard."

"How?" I asked.

"Whitlock called him this morning. He's headed over to talk to him now. How'd it go when you met with him?"

"We talked about the allegations that were brought to my attention."

"And? What did he have to say for himself?"

I spent the next several minutes giving Foley a recap of the conversation I'd had with Warren.

When I finished, he said, "It's refreshing to question someone and have them respond the way he did. What you told him couldn't have been easy for him to hear, whether it's true or not."

"If what I said upset him, he did a great job of not showing it. He looked … well, hurt to hear how Margot felt about some of their interactions together."

"After talking to him, what's your honest opinion?"

"I want to believe he's innocent, incapable of harming Margot, let alone killing her," I said. "He seems like a devoted husband, and the way he was with his wife when I was there suggests they have a good relationship."

"I'm sensing a *but* in there somewhere."

"It's like the guy could pass gas, and everyone around him would smell nothing but a garden of roses."

"Ehh, gross, but I get your meaning."

"His responses to my questions were perfect, but after I left, I started to wonder if they were too perfect. I'll be interested to hear what Whitlock thinks once he's spoken with him."

"Who came to you with allegations against Coach Warren?"

"I promised I'd keep their identities a secret," I said.

"I give you my word I'll keep it to myself. Won't tell a soul, but I want to know."

"A couple of girls on the volleyball team. They were friends of Margot's."

"And did they believe he'd done anything wrong?"

"They both like him, and they've never had an experience like Margot had."

Foley put his truck into gear and nodded. "Thanks for confiding in me. I expect I'll see you tonight at Sunday dinner?"

I shot him a sarcastic grin. "I can't wait."

He met my sarcasm and raised me with a smirk of his own, saying, "Me either."

30

I pulled into the Boathouse Diner's parking lot at one o'clock on the dot. Giovanni met me at my car, reached for my hand, and we walked together into the diner. As the hostess escorted us to our seats, someone called my name. I glanced back and saw Sebastian's parents. They were smiling and waving us over to their table.

"Someone's trying hard to get your attention," Giovanni said.

"Sean and Meredith Chandler. They're the parents of Margot's ex-boyfriend, Sebastian."

"I see."

Taking the rest of the day off would have to wait.

"I'll keep it brief, and then we'll slip away," I said.

We made our way over to their table, and Sean gestured to the chairs across from them, saying, "We'd love it if the two of you joined us."

"We appreciate the offer," I said, "but—"

"Please," Meredith said. "We've just been talking about … well, we were talking about contacting you, and here you are. It seems like fate, doesn't it?"

It seemed like an unfortunate coincidence.

I introduced Giovanni, and we sat down.

"Why were you thinking about contacting me?" I asked.

"We wanted to talk to you about Sebastian," Sean said.

"What about him?"

"He's been so distant ever since Margot died," Sean said. "He's never been the talkative type, to be honest, but he's not talking much at all."

"He's not eating either," Meredith said. "We're worried. Sebastian mentioned he's seen you a few times this week. Has he said anything noteworthy to you?"

"We've talked, and I'd say he's struggling right now. Processing Margot's death is going to be difficult. He needs time to heal. I wouldn't worry too much about him being quieter than usual. He's been spending time with Bronte, and that's a start."

"It is," Sean said. "We were glad to hear they're speaking again. We stopped by to see Dr. Rae this morning, to ask if there was anything we could do for her. Sebastian was there. He didn't say much to us, of course. But he seemed all right, better than he has been."

A waiter approached the table and offered to get us something to drink. Sean ordered a beer, and Meredith ordered red wine. Hoping to break away from them sooner than later, Giovanni and I stuck with the glasses of water the waiter had just set on the table.

"What has Sebastian said to you, if you don't mind me asking," Meredith said.

I considered how to respond without betraying his trust.

In my opinion, his mother's behavior was one of the main reasons he'd been distant. Entering his room during the press conference like she had and trying to get him to talk about his feelings before he was ready was a bad idea. To top things off, she'd gone a step further, turning the press conference into a spectacle by gossiping to her friends. She lacked consideration for what her son was going through, prompting me to offer some unsolicited advice.

"Sebastian and I have talked," I said. "He needs time to deal with his feelings on his own. I know how much you both want him to open up, but have you ever considered that he's not ready to talk to you about anything yet?"

"I get what you're saying," Meredith said. "It's just that I'd rather him let out the feelings he's repressing sooner than later. Until he does, he won't be able to move on."

"Maybe he's *not* ready to move on."

"It's a valid point," Sean said.

"How's your investigation going?" Meredith asked. "Are you getting anywhere?"

I was beginning to wonder whether they'd called me over to talk about their son or whether talking about him was a stepping stone to get information about Margot's case.

I took a moment to think about what to say next. Anything I told Meredith would be passed along; I had no doubt. I considered saying nothing. Then I thought about it from a different perspective. Maybe it was time to turn up the pressure around town, fuel the rumor mill, and see where it led.

And I knew just the thing to say.

"Bronte found a note in her car the other day," I said. "It was written in Margot's handwriting, and I believe it was placed in Bronte's car on the day Margot went missing."

Meredith leaned in, her eyes wide with wonder.

It was just the reaction I wanted.

"Well …" she said. "What did the note say?"

"Margot was keeping a secret, one she hadn't shared with anyone, and she wanted Bronte's advice. She also mentioned there was more to her breakup with Sebastian than people knew."

Sean and Meredith exchanged confused glances.

"We were under the impression they broke up over what happened the night of the party," Sean said. "What other reason could there be? Have you talked to Sebastian about it?"

"I have. He has no idea what Margot meant in her note."

The waiter brought Sean and Meredith's drinks, and I glanced at Giovanni, indicating now was a good time to make a move.

"It was nice to meet you both," Giovanni said. "We need to be going."

"Sure," Sean said. "Thanks for your time."

"Yes, thank you," Meredith said. "If there's anything we can do to help, Georgiana, you be sure to let us know."

We stood, and I had the urge to get one last comment in before we walked away.

"Margot may not have gotten the chance to tell her secret before she died, but I have no doubt I will figure it out," I said. "When I do, I believe I'll know who killed her and why."

31

It had been a couple of hours since my run-in with Sebastian's parents, and I imagined Meredith had speed-dialed all her friends by now to dish out the news I'd given her.

I stopped by the grocery store to pick up a few things for a cheese board I was bringing to tonight's dinner. As I left the store, I saw Sebastian sitting in his truck in the parking lot. I walked over, using my knuckle to tap on the driver's-side window. The gesture startled him, and he dropped the cell phone he'd been staring at on the floor. He leaned down to pick it up from the floorboard, then rolled his window down.

"You know, I'm starting to feel like you're following me," I said. "Seems like wherever I go, here you are."

He wasn't amused by my comment.

"I could say the same thing about you," he said. "It's not like I knew you were going to be here. I'm waiting for Bronte. She's inside, grabbing a few things for her mom."

It was a small store, and I hadn't seen her.

"I saw your parents earlier today," I said.

He sighed. "Yeah, I know. My mom texted me. Why did you tell her about the note?"

"No offense, but when it comes to spreading news around town, your mother excels at it. I figured I'd mention the note and see what happens when it gets people talking. Who knows? Maybe someone will come forward with new information and tell me something I don't already know."

"If someone knows Margot's secret, wouldn't they have spoken up by now?"

"I wish it worked that way, but most of the time, it doesn't."

"What do you mean?"

"It takes a lot of prodding to get people to open up at times, even when they know it's the right thing to do," I said. "Take you, for example."

"What about me?"

"You didn't open up to me right away, and I'm convinced there are things you still haven't told me. It's not a judgment; it's an observation. You're a private person. I am too. It's not always easy to talk about your life or to answer hard questions with someone you don't know."

He glanced out the window. "I've never been good at … you know, talking to most people. Or my parents."

"I get it, believe me. Your parents asked me about you because they know I've seen you a few times. They're concerned about how you're doing."

"I've told them a hundred times, I'm fine. I wish they'd stop asking."

He may have said he was fine, but he bit down on his lip when he said it, and his eyes began to water.

"Are you fine?" I asked.

Another pause, and then, "No … I don't want to talk about it, and I don't want to talk about *her*. It's too hard."

He wiped his eyes on his shirt sleeve, clearing his throat several times as he tried to regain control of his emotions. It made me feel awful, like I'd added to his pain somehow.

"I wish I could say it's going to get easier, that the pain you're feeling right now will ease," I said. "Grieving the death of someone you cared about isn't easy."

He sniffled a few times and said, "Yeah, I know."

I sensed he wanted to be alone, so I said, "I … ahh, I need to run, unless you want me to stay a little longer. Because I can."

"Nah, I'm good." He peeked inside my bag. "What's with all the cheese?"

"I'm having family dinner tonight at my mother's house. I'm in charge of the cheese board."

"My parents want to have family dinner tonight too. My mom thinks we can all celebrate the holiday and pretend like nothing else is going on. I can't pretend, and I won't."

"Will you go home for dinner?"

"Nope. Bronte said I can hang with them tonight."

Meredith may not have been mother of the year, but she loved her son.

"Have you thought about talking to your mom about how you feel?" I asked.

"No."

"I won't tell you what to do or what not to do, but maybe if you sent your mom a simple text, telling her what you just told me, she'd understand."

"I doubt it."

"Think about it." I fished a business card out of my handbag and offered it to him. "And hey, we haven't known each other long, but if you ever want to talk about anything, give me a call."

32

I sat in my usual chair at my mother's dinner table, so stuffed with food, I was certain standing would be difficult. I glanced around the table, staring into the faces of those around me, and I felt grateful to be there, spending the evening with those I cared about most. And though I grumbled at times about attending family events, I loved it when we came together the way we were tonight.

Giovanni and I were joined at the table by my mother and my stepfather, Harvey. My sister, Phoebe, was seated across from me next to Foley, and my niece, Lark, was to the other side of her. My brother, Nathan, had flown in from somewhere abroad, where his job as a marine wildlife photographer often took him. And then there was Simone, sitting next to her husband, Paul, my other brother. At the end of the table was my Aunt Laura. She was seated beside Whitlock. I'd had my eye on them throughout dinner, and I believed I'd seen a little flirting going on between the two of them.

"Well, I cannot believe it," my mother said. "We've managed to get through an entire meal without one word mentioned about the case you're working on, Georgiana."

And yet, she was bringing it up now.

I wondered why.

"I know how much you dislike me discussing homicide investigations at the dinner table," I said.

"You're right. I don't like it at all. I must say … this one is different."

"Different how?" I asked.

"Half the people at this table are involved in Margot's case, and Dr. Rae is … well, my doctor, and Laura's, and Simone's, and yours, Georgiana. I've known Dr. Rae for years. Many of us have. So just this once, I wouldn't mind hearing about what's happening with the investigation. For starters, why on earth is it taking so long to find the person responsible for killing her daughter?"

I glanced at Foley and Whitlock, hoping they'd say a few words. The expressions on their faces told me they had zero interest in being the first to speak up.

"It's been a week, Mom," I said. "Cases like this take time."

She wagged a finger at me. "For some, not for you. You have a track record of closing your investigations in a week's time, do you not?"

"We just discovered her … uhh, you know, two days ago."

"I'm aware, but surely there are people you suspect."

I turned toward Lark, who was clutching her stuffed unicorn a lot tighter than she had been a few minutes ago. Given she was nine years old, I wasn't about to discuss suspects and other aspects of the case in front of her.

"We should move this conversation to the game room," I said.

"Excellent idea," Harvey added.

"I'll clear the table," Phoebe said. "Those of you who want to talk, go and talk."

Phoebe stood and began gathering plates. Giovanni joined her, followed by my brothers and my aunt. My mother, Harvey, Simone, Foley, Whitlock, and I reconvened in the game room, taking seats on the sectional sofa. Over the next several minutes, Foley and Whitlock gave an overview of the investigation on their end, and

Simone and I talked about what we'd been doing on ours.

I was hoping to avoid talking about suspects in the case, but there was no getting around it. My mother pushed until we relented and offered a few small details about those we'd been talking to in the past week.

When we finished, she wasted no time piping up with her opinions.

She stood in front of us like she was on stage and said, "I've watched enough episodes of *Murder, She Wrote* to know the suspects who seem innocent are almost always guilty. I suggest you speak to this Coach Warren fellow again. I'll just bet Margot's note and the secret she was keeping has to do with him. There's more to the story between those two. I feel it in my bones. Yes, yes. It makes perfect sense. My money's on him."

For a moment, we all sat there, looking at each other and saying nothing.

No one wanted to be the one to discredit what she'd said for fear of the backlash they'd receive if they did.

Harvey seemed to sense our hesitation.

He looked at my mother and said, "Well, Darlene, you bring up some good points. I'm sure they'll take your feelings about the coach into consideration."

"Of course, they will," my mother said. "And why not make haste? Why not go to this coach person's house this very moment and give him another grilling? You put the screws to him hard enough, I bet he'll drop the innocent act and you'll get a full confession."

"It's Christmas Eve, Mom," I said. "It can wait."

"Are you suggesting Dr. Rae should wait too?" my mother asked. "Every second this case isn't solved is another second the good doctor lives without an ounce of closure. She deserves answers. If you can give them to her, why wouldn't you?"

"She will have answers soon enough," I said. "I know you're worried about her and what she's going through. So are we. I need you to trust me, to trust us, and that we are doing everything we can. Please."

Before my mother had the chance to respond, Harvey looked at Foley and said, "You mentioned another suspect a few minutes ago, Isaac Turner. The name is familiar to me. I feel like I've spoken to him before, some time back, before I retired."

Foley nodded. "You're right. You met him when he was a lot younger. I located an old file on him. When he was in middle school, he took a pair of scissors and lopped off a big chunk of one of his female classmate's hair."

Harvey nodded. "Oh, yes, I remember now. The principal called, and I went to the school and talked to Isaac. He claimed the girl wouldn't stop making fun of him, and he wanted to teach her a lesson."

He wanted to teach her a lesson.

Had he wanted to teach Margot one too?

Just when I thought my mother would make another case for Coach Warren's guilt, she surprised me by saying, "Perhaps you need to speak to both men again."

Her tone had changed, becoming a lot calmer than it had been moments before. I had to hand it to Harvey. He knew just what to say in situations like these.

Whitlock stood and said, "Well, folks, getting together tonight has been an absolute delight. The food was incredible, Darlene. Thank you for including me in the festivities this evening. I'd stay longer, but this old-timer knows when it's best to call it a night."

"We've enjoyed your company," my mother said. "You have an open invitation to join us for Sunday dinner anytime."

Whitlock offered his gratitude one last time and shot me a wink. "Care to walk me out?"

I nodded, and we went to the kitchen, where the rest of the family was working putting away food and washing dishes. Phoebe handed Whitlock a to-go container full of various items, and I escorted him outside.

As the door closed behind us, I said, "You and Aunt Laura sure were chatty at the dinner table tonight. Have you ever thought about asking her on a date?"

He grinned and said, "What makes you think I haven't?"

"Oh, well, good for you. She likes your company. I can tell."

"Listen, the reason I asked you to walk me out is because there's something I didn't mention. I love your mother, but she doesn't need to know everything, and I also wanted to speak to you first."

"About what?"

"When I arrived at Warren's house today, his wife, Cass, was leaving."

"When you say *leaving*, do you mean to run errands, or …?"

He shook his head. "She put a suitcase in the car. Five minutes later, she was gone."

"Did Cass say where she was going?"

"Not to me. I questioned Warren about it, and he said they'd gotten into an argument, and she'd decided to spend Christmas Day with her sister."

"Did he tell you what the argument was about?" I asked.

"He did not."

"When I was at their house they were all over each other for the first part of my visit, and then when I brought up the allegations I'd heard about Warren, Cass' mood changed. She got it in her mind that everyone in town has been spreading rumors about Warren, and she worried he might lose his job over it. Warren tried to downplay the situation, and it didn't work. Cass felt like he wasn't taking it seriously enough and she shut herself in the bedroom."

Whitlock opened the car door and turned to face me. "After you left, I'm guessing the argument got worse. I arrived, and by then, she'd decided to leave."

"Did Warren seem upset over it?" I asked.

"He did, but not as much as he could have been. I get the impression he's passive by nature. Everything seems to roll right off the guy, even when he's accused of being inappropriate with one of his students."

Whitlock got in the car and set the to-go container on the passenger seat.

"Aside from Warren's lackadaisical attitude, what do you think about him?" I asked.

"Seems like a nice guy to me. Doesn't strike me as the type of person who would murder someone, but all types of people commit murder, even passive ones. Oh, and one more thing … we looked over the surveillance video from the night Sebastian was supposed to meet with Margot. It checks out."

"He was there, the entire time?"

"He arrived and departed when he said he did. Doesn't mean he couldn't have killed her and found a way to get to the restaurant to give himself an alibi."

"I'd say he's innocent," I said. "I've felt that way for a few days now. Plus, when you consider the timetable, and the fact Margot was driven to the hiking trail and what happened there, I don't see how he could have made it back in time."

"I agree."

It was a relief to cross Sebastian off my list.

One down.

Several more to go.

33

I woke up Christmas morning and decided to push the pause button on the investigation and spend the day with Giovanni and Luka instead. It allowed me the time I needed to reflect on where the case was so far and what to do next. It wasn't easy taking a day off, not even when it was a holiday. But sometimes taking a step back helped me see a new path forward. I spent the day relaxing, clearing my head, and making a game plan for the week. By seven, I was in bed.

The following afternoon was Margot's funeral. Many of the town's locals had gathered to show their support for Rae and her family. It made me stop and think about what a tight-knit community we were, and even more so in times of crisis.

I'd been inside the chapel for less than ten seconds before an all-too-familiar voice could be heard, shouting over all those who had gathered.

"Yoo-hoo, Georgiana. Over here."

I squinted, staring through the crowd until my eyes came to rest on my mother and stepfather who were seated in the third row. To ensure I'd heard her, she stood up, waving at me with both hands like we hadn't seen each other in years. As I walked toward her, my stepfather placed a hand on my mother's arm and leaned toward her, no doubt whispering a suggestion that she sit back down. Harvey had never been one for a spectacle, which proved to be difficult at times, given my mother's boisterous, over-the-top personality.

My mother shrugged Harvey off and bounded my way, wrapping her arms around me in a tight embrace.

"Well, my goodness, I didn't notice at Sunday dinner, but you're turning into a slip of a thing," she said. "Have you been eating? Have you been getting enough sleep? I should say not, by the looks of it."

Gee, thanks, Mom.

Hello to you too.

"You saw how much I had to eat at your house the other night," I said.

She took a step back and frowned. "Just because you had a full plate on Sunday doesn't mean you're eating the rest of the time. I'm concerned about your wellbeing."

"I'm fine, Mom. We should take a seat. The service is about to start."

She swished a hand through the air, tipping her head toward the chapel door. "People are still filing in. The service won't begin for at least five or ten minutes, I'd say. Come, come. We saved you a seat."

Sitting in the third row where I couldn't observe all that was going on around me wasn't how I'd wanted things to go. I started to think of ways around it, and then I spotted the perfect backup plan.

"I'll be right back, Mom," I said.

"I don't understand. You just said we needed to sit down. Where are you going?"

Without providing an answer, I made a beeline toward the back of the chapel. Simone had just walked in, and I wanted to catch her while I had the chance. She'd ditched her usual concert T-shirt, blazer, jeans, and Dr. Martens, and was dressed in a navy suit and matching stilettos. Aside from her wedding day, it was the most formal attire I'd ever seen her wear.

"I wasn't sure if you were going to be here," I said. "I'm glad you came. Harvey and my mother are here too."

"Yeah," Simone said. "I tried calling you, but you didn't answer, and I knew I'd find you here."

I removed my phone from my handbag and glanced at the screen. "Sorry, I forgot to take it off mute when I got up this morning. Listen, I need a favor."

"Yeah, sure. What's up?"

"My mother wants me to sit up front with her, which means I won't be able to hang back and observe everyone during the services. I need you to be my eyes and ears. I'd like you to look around, get a feel for anyone or anything out of the ordinary."

"You bet. I need a task to help pass the time. Funerals give me the heebie-jeebies."

"Oh? I didn't know."

"It's all right. I'm here because we're working this case together. I was hoping to catch up with you at your mother's house the other night, but we didn't get the chance to be alone. I still need to tell you about the conversation I had with Kaia."

"Let's get together after the funeral is over," I said. "You can talk to me about Kaia, and I'll fill you in on all that's happened since we last spoke."

She moved a hand to her hip. "It's a deal … on one condition."

"What's the condition?"

"As soon as the funeral ends, we get the hell out of here and grab a drink somewhere. I always need one after a funeral … well, one or five, give or take."

I'd never been much of a day drinker, or in this case, an afternoon drinker, and I had no interest in starting now. There were also other things I wanted to accomplish today. But as I looked at Simone, there was a nervousness in her I wasn't used to seeing—a vast difference from her usual confident, outgoing self.

I lifted a finger. "One drink."

"I'll take it."

I smiled and turned, picking up the pace as I spotted the pastor making his way to the pulpit. To top it off, the expression on my mother's face was one of disappointment, which made me feel even worse. I scooted in next to her, hoping she wouldn't say anything, but knowing she would.

"It's about time," she said. "You and your sister-in-law were back there prattling on for ages."

In truth, it had been a few minutes, but I kept quiet.

As the pastor began his opening remarks, I focused on what I could see from my position. To the far right, I spotted Rae in the front row. Bronte was beside her with her arm draped around her shoulders. On the other side of Rae was a man who resembled her. I guessed it was her brother, Jay. I watched him for a time, noticing his eyes were darting around, looking at various people in attendance. His gaze met mine, and I acknowledged him with a nod. He nodded back, offering a slight grin like Rae had told him about me.

Sitting in the row behind Rae was Grant, his attention focused on Bronte. His expression was grim, like *he* should be the one comforting Rae, not *her*. I wondered whether Rae had spoken to him again or seen him since I visited her. I also wondered why he was in the second row instead of the first.

Sitting right in front of me was Sebastian, alongside his parents. As soon as the pastor began talking he'd leaned forward, facing the floor, his hands flattened on both sides of his face like blinders. Given how much of a private person he was, I imagined he was trying to shield everyone from seeing his emotions.

I craned my head back to get a look at the people in the rows behind me, and was met with an elbow jab to my side.

"I know what you're doing, Georgiana," my mother whispered. "Now is not the time."

"Now is the perfect time," I said.

She shook her head, huffing a sigh loud enough for those around us to hear. Meredith glanced back, glaring at me like we needed to keep quiet. As much as I didn't appreciate her disdainful expression, she was right. We shouldn't have been chitchatting while the service was taking place.

The pastor finished his opening remarks and invited Rae to say a few words. She spoke with eloquence, her words so powerful, most in attendance were moved to tears. Next to speak was Bronte who recalled some of her favorite moments she'd had with her sister over the years. Her words were soft and heartfelt at first, but before she finished, they changed to words of anger, as she proclaimed her sister would not die in vain. She closed with a promise, a vow to never to stop looking for her sister's killer until he was found.

As Bronte returned to her seat, the congregation went quiet, a feeling of awkwardness spreading throughout the chapel. The pastor returned to the pulpit, saying anyone who wanted to speak could now do so. I expected a line to form, but it seemed no one wanted to go first.

My mother leaned over, whispering, "You're working on the case. A few words, perhaps?"

"I don't think it's my place."

"It's everyone's place if you have something to say. Since when are you at a loss for words?"

She'd said it like she'd meant it as a compliment, but it wasn't one, and though speaking at Margot's funeral wasn't on my agenda, I didn't want the service to end like this—with no other family or friends stepping up to speak on her behalf. To add to the tension I was feeling, I'd never been good at enduring long moments of silence. Every second that passed felt like a minute, and with it a sense of pressure mounting, like it was up to me to do something, even though it wasn't.

I was about to stand when something unexpected happened. Sebastian got up—the last person I expected to speak on Margot's behalf. For a moment, I thought his intention had been to exit the chapel without offering any remarks, but I was wrong. He approached the pulpit, standing there for a time, his head bowed, tears flowing. His parents exchanged a worried glance like they were trying to decide if one of them should come to his rescue.

Keeping his head down, Sebastian began speaking.

"I've known Margot since we were kids," he said. "Back then, I always thought she was … well, I didn't notice her much, to be honest. And even though we had a lot of the same teachers at school, I didn't say a lot to her over the years. Last year we were assigned to do a science project together. She came over to my house, and as we sat there, and talked, and laughed, I realized I should have gotten to know her a lot earlier. She was a beautiful person, on the inside and out. She loved animals. She loved helping people. She loved making people happy. And for a while, I'd like to believe … to believe … she loved … *me*."

He choked out those last words and went quiet. It seemed like he was finished until he didn't return to his seat. He just stood there. After some time passed, the pastor approached Sebastian. He leaned over, whispered in his ear, and Sebastian whispered back. The pastor nodded and sat back down again.

More silence followed, and then Sebastian looked up for the first time, but he didn't look into the crowd. He looked at me.

"What happened to Margot should have never happened," he said. "And I want to say … I need to say that what happened to her was wrong. How could a person hurt her the way they did? How could someone leave her out there, cold, and alone, and scared, because she must have been scared. I'm just so … I'm so angry, and I want to kill the person who did this, because they killed her."

His eyes closed, and he sagged to the ground. Rae shot up, rushing to his side. Sean, was next, sprinting toward his son. He knelt, cradling Sebastian's head in his hands as he spoke to him, trying to get him to open his eyes. Soon, others joined in, creating a circle around him.

Gasps and chatter were heard from onlookers wondering what had happened to Sebastian. A few minutes later, Rae told everyone that Sebastian had fainted. He was going to be fine.

From behind, I heard laughter, followed by, "He's trying hard to make himself look innocent, isn't he?"

I turned around, glaring at Isaac, who had spoken loud enough for most of the attendees sitting in our section to overhear.

Everything in me told me to remain quiet.

I did not.

"Shut your mouth," I said. "Show some respect for the family."

"Oh, hey, Detective," he said. "Bet you're shocked to see me here. Bet you hoped they'd lock me up so you could tell all your buddies you solved the case. Get a nice pat on the back. I got three words for ya: Not. Enough. Evidence. Or maybe I should say, *no* evidence."

I pictured myself jumping over the pews and tackling him. Harvey noticed the look in my eye, and he reached out, giving my leg a gentle pat.

I took a breath.

And then another.

"If you cared about Margot at all, grow up and don't disgrace her funeral service any further, Isaac," I said.

In that moment, my mother realized the Isaac I was talking to was the same Isaac we'd told her about at Sunday dinner. She turned, eyes narrowed as she said, "Young man, you are out of order. If you do not shut your trap this moment, I will have you removed from the building."

Isaac opened his mouth to speak, and his mother looked at him, saying, "Please. This is not the time."

He nodded, and I rose from my seat and walked toward Sebastian. Bending down, I tapped Sean on the shoulder and said, "How's he doing?"

Sean nodded. "He'll be all right."

Sebastian glanced up at Rae, repeating the words, "I'm sorry," over and over again.

"No need to apologize," she said. "What you said meant a lot to me, and it would have meant a lot to Margot."

34

"Well, ho-lee crap," Simone said. "Never expected anyone to pass out. Woke me right up."

We were sitting beside each other at The Untamed Shrew, our local watering hole. Simone was sipping on a Cosmopolitan, and I was staring at my glass of rosé, reliving the highlights of the funeral service.

"I've been thinking a lot about what Sebastian said before he fainted," I said. "He's one of the most introverted people I've ever met. It took a lot for him to get up in front of everyone and say what he did. I can't stop replaying it in my mind."

She turned toward me. "What are you thinking?"

"When Sebastian got to the part of his speech where he said he was angry and wanted to kill the person who murdered Margot, he looked right at me. It was almost like he was trying to tell me something."

"Maybe it was a warning."

"What do you mean?"

"A warning like—you better find Margot's killer before he does."

It was possible.

If he came to the wake, I'd ask him about it.

"What did Kaia say when you talked to her?" I asked.

Simone moved a hand to her hip. "Before I talk about the conversation I had with her, is there anything else you need me to do for you today?"

"No, why?"

She waved a hand in the air, summoning the bartender. He walked over, smiled at her, and she said, "I'll have another Cosmopolitan, please."

He nodded and walked away.

"Can I ask you something?" I said.

"Let me guess. You want to know why I drink after I attend a funeral."

"If you don't mind me asking, yes."

She polished off her Cosmopolitan and said, "I lost my older sister when I was twelve years old. She had brain cancer. All these years later, I still think about the day she died whenever I'm at a funeral. I wish I didn't keep reliving it, but I do."

"I had no idea. I'm sorry. Does my brother know?"

"He does. He offered to pick me up."

"I could drive you home."

"He's already on the way. Do you want to know something? My sister is the reason I became a detective. She wanted to be a police officer when she grew up. I became one as a way to honor her life."

"You are honoring her life," I said.

The bartender returned, clearing Simone's first drink before setting down the second.

"Enough heavy talk," Simone said. "Let's talk about Kaia."

"Did she have anything enlightening to say?"

"She sure did. Get this—she was driving home last week, and she passed Isaac. He saw her and turned around and started following her. When she pulled over, he approached her car and asked her out on a date."

"After what he did at Sebastian's house, he had the nerve to ask her out? Wow, that's ballsy, even for him. What did she say?"

"She asked him to admit that he'd tricked her on the night of the party, and he admitted it. He even said he set her up so he could make a move on Margot. He started laughing and said he couldn't understand why everyone was so upset about it. To him, it was just a joke."

"How did Kaia respond?" I asked.

"She told him it wasn't funny. His actions hurt people. Isaac laughed and told her to chill out. She flipped him the finger and sped off."

"Good for her. Do you know what day she spoke to him?"

"Yep, the day after Margot went missing. Now it's your turn to fill me in on what you've learned since I saw you last."

I spent the next several minutes telling Simone about everyone I'd interviewed over the last few days.

When I finished, she said, "Let me see if I have this right. Your current suspects are Rae's boyfriend, Grant, and Isaac, and Coach Warren, who I feel like you don't want to be guilty of murder."

"That's my roster to date. I'm heading over to the wake in a few minutes. I hope to speak to Grant and Sebastian if they're there. Then I'm going to check in on Coach Warren. He skipped the funeral service like he said he would. I'd like to know whether he's talked to his wife since she left the house."

"And I'd like to know if he's as innocent as he seems. In my experience, no one can be as passive as he comes off all the time. It's not realistic."

Simone finished her Cosmopolitan and excused herself to use the restroom. My brother entered the bar a couple of minutes later, and I waved him over.

He took a seat next to me and said, "How's she doing?"

"She's all right. We talked about why funerals are hard for her."

"I'm glad she told you. Thanks for being here with her, sis."

"Any time."

Simone returned from the restroom, and I hopped off the barstool, and we said our goodbyes. The wake was starting in ten minutes, and I didn't want to miss a moment of it.

35

The wake was a drop-in affair, and so far, only a few people had arrived, which was a good thing. Through Rae's front window, I saw Grant standing by himself in the living room. He was holding a glass of beer and glancing at a series of photos of Margot on display on a shelf over the fireplace.

I made my way over to him.

"How are you doing?" I asked.

His eyes remained on a photo of Margot as he said, "Why? Are you here to interrogate me again?"

"I'm here to show my support for Rae and Bronte."

He turned toward me, the expression on his face one of suspicion. "You don't fool me. I've been around you enough this last week to know you're always on the clock, scrutinizing everyone from every angle."

"I'd like to think there's more to me than what you see. You're entitled to your opinion. I just don't happen to share it."

He paused and said, "Hell, maybe I am being too hard on you. I know you have a job to do."

It wasn't an apology, but it was something.

Grant swallowed back some beer and shifted his focus to Rae who was engaged in a conversation with a couple in the kitchen.

"How are things between the two of you?" I asked.

"They're not. We broke up."

"When?"

"Last night."

"What happened?"

"She invited me over, sat me down, and said she doesn't have time to concentrate on us right now with everything else going on in her life. Ask me, her kid put her up to it. She was lurking around during the conversation. Didn't say two words to me the entire time I was here."

"Rae doesn't strike me as the type of person who would allow Bronte to influence her in such a way, not even under these circumstances."

"I don't know how else to make sense of it. Two weeks ago, we were talking about taking the next step in our relationship, and now, we're finished."

Two weeks ago, Rae's life hadn't been turned upside down. And now, here we were talking about *his* feelings about the breakup. He had yet to say one word about Margot or to express sympathy for Rae and what she was going through. All he seemed to care about was himself and how *his life* had been impacted since Margot died.

I allowed it, if for no other reason than to see what else I could get out of him.

"Once Rae has had time to process what's happened, maybe the two of you will find a way back to each other," I said.

"No, we won't."

"Why not?"

"Because I've had enough of this town. I'm moving. I'm getting as far away from here as I can."

"When's the move?" I asked.

"This weekend. Putting my place up for sale tomorrow."

It was unexpected, and it made me question if there was another reason for his swift departure.

"Where are you moving?" I asked.

"Reno."

"Why Reno?"

"My brother lives there. He's offered me a management position with his construction company."

"When did you make the decision?" I asked.

"Today, during the funeral when I was made to feel like a third wheel. Our relationship hasn't even been over for twenty-four hours, and Rae is already distancing herself from me."

"Have you told her yet?"

He shrugged. "What's the point?"

"If there's no point, why are you even here?"

He drank the remainder of his beer and set the empty glass down in front of a photo of Margot, which seemed like a strange place to put it given there was a side table within reach.

For a moment, he didn't say anything, and then he sighed and said, "You know something? You're right. I don't know what I'm doing here. Maybe I was hoping Rae and I could talk, and once I told her I was moving, she'd say something to change my mind. I'm an idiot, a total idiot, and I'm wasting my time."

Grant started for the front door, a move Rae noticed. She excused herself from the couple she'd been talking to and went outside. I stood in the living room trying to decide whether to remain there or to join them. It was possible they needed a moment alone together. Then again, his temper was unpredictable. Perhaps it wasn't a good idea for them to be alone in this moment when she had a house full of guests. With that in mind, I headed outside.

As soon as Grant saw me, he shook his head and said, "What is it with you?"

"I know how upset you are right now, and I just wanted to make sure Rae is all right."

"She's fine," he said. "Why wouldn't she be? What do you think I'm going to do—murder her for breaking up with me last night and ignoring me all day today?"

"You think I was ignoring you?" Rae asked.

"Sure seemed like it to me."

She raised her hands in front of her. "Wow, Grant. I thought you knew me better. Or maybe I just wanted to believe you did. I can't ... I can't deal with this right now."

She turned and went back inside.

Grant huffed a slew of swear words and walked to his truck.

I almost went after him, but I didn't.

Someone else had just parked in the driveway—someone I wanted to talk to even more than Grant.

36

I stepped off the front porch onto the driveway and said, "I'm surprised to see you here."

"I'm not staying," Coach Warren said. "I just came to drop off some flowers for Rae. Have you been able to speak to Bronte?"

I shook my head. "There's been a lot going on. I haven't seen her since I talked to you last."

"Where is she right now?"

"I don't know," I said. "She could be in her room."

He tapped a shoe on the ground, thinking. "Do you think I should go inside, say a few words to Rae?"

"I don't know. It's up to you."

"I can't decide. I'm starting to think that maybe coming here wasn't a good idea."

In my opinion, it was a great one.

I had a few more questions to ask.

"I heard your wife left after I talked to you," I said.

"Yeah ... she did. She'll be back. She does this sometimes."

"Your wife leaves sometimes? Why?"

"She thinks I'm not concerned enough about serious issues when they come up in our life. It's my personality, I guess. I don't want to upset her, but what am I supposed to do? Pretend I'm as upset as she is even though I'm not? I'm a glass half-full type of guy. Things always work themselves out."

Warren was perhaps the most passive man I'd ever met, so passive I was still having a hard time picturing him molesting and killing Margot. I thought about Skye and Elle, and how highly they'd spoken about him when they came to see me.

I didn't know what to believe anymore.

I ran my hands up and down my arms, realizing how cool it had become since the sun had gone down. I tilted my face toward the sky. It looked like it might start snowing. Warren handed me the flowers he'd been holding, removed his coat, and wrapped it around me.

"You don't need to … I'm fine," I said.

"You're not fine. You're freezing."

Freezing until a hot flash kicks in.

"Look, I … I need to say something," he said.

"I'm listening."

"I've had some time to think about what Margot said and about how uncomfortable I made her feel. Maybe the hug lasted too long. What can I say? I'm a hugger. I suppose I haven't thought about the fact that it might make others uncomfortable. I'll be aware of it in the future, and I'll also have an open conversation from now on with my students, so they know they can talk to me if they have any concerns."

"Good idea. Is there anything else?"

"The private session I had with Margot. I can see now that it wasn't a good idea to put myself into that kind of situation. If I pressed my body against Margot's during our coaching session, I wouldn't have even realized it at the time. My sole focus would have been on the instructions I was giving her."

His sentiments seemed genuine, but I found myself questioning everything about him.

"Seems like you've given Margot's concerns a lot of thought," I said.

"I have, and I want to be honest with everyone about it so this never happens again. To start, I've written letters to Rae and Bronte, explaining myself, but also apologizing for making Margot feel the way I did."

I glanced at the front door. People were starting to depart, which meant our private conversation wouldn't be able to continue much longer.

Warren pulled two envelopes out of his pocket and handed them to me. "Will you give Rae this letter along with the flowers, and will you give Bronte the other letter?"

"I will."

I removed the coat he'd wrapped around me and handed it back to him. "It's not often I meet people like you. I mean no offense when I say this, but you seem so genuine, it's almost hard for me to believe you are."

"It's not the first time someone has said that to me," he said.

And something told me it wouldn't be the last.

37

found Bronte in her room, sitting on her bed, with headphones over her ears. I waved from the doorway, and she pulled the headphones off, setting them down beside her.

"I can't take people anymore today," she said. "The funeral wiped me out."

"I get it. I'm not trying to bug you."

"You're not. Come in."

I entered her room and took a seat at her desk.

She grabbed her cell phone, looked at it, and set it on the nightstand.

"I have a letter for you," I said. "It's from Coach Warren. He asked me to give it to you, and before you say anything, I don't know what it says. I have an idea, though."

"Uhh, oh … kay. Why did he write me a letter?"

"I talked to him about Margot, like I said I would. He said he felt bad for making her feel the way he did. I'm guessing the letter he wrote you is an explanation and an apology."

"Do you think he's innocent?"

"I don't know. I wish I did."

She grunted, "When will you know?" and then leaned against her headboard. "Sorry. That was rude. I'm tired."

"I'm as frustrated as you are that her case hasn't been solved yet."

"Yeah ... well, I don't want his stupid letter."

"I get it. Tell you what ... I'll set it here on the desk, and you do whatever you want with it. Trash it, shred it, light it on fire ... whatever you think is best."

She grinned. "You're kinda savage, aren't you?"

"I'd say I'm a bit more than *kinda* savage. I try to rein it in when I can."

She reached for her cell phone once more, looked at it, and set it back down again.

"Are you waiting to hear from someone?" I asked.

"Yeah ... Sebastian."

"Is he coming over? I haven't seen him or his parents since I arrived."

"Who knows, at this point? Last night he said he'd hang out with me while the wake was going on, so we could do our own thing. I've been messaging him ever since the funeral ended. He's not responding."

"Do you think he's embarrassed because he fainted earlier today?"

"I'm sure he is, but here's the thing— it's not like him to leave me hanging, or anyone. If he says he's going to be somewhere, he's there. He's the least flaky person I know."

"Have you called him?"

"Yep. Goes to voicemail. I don't get it. I was going to drive to his place, but I don't want to leave my mom until everyone's gone."

I glanced at my watch.

The wake was over in forty minutes.

Again, my mind wandered to what Sebastian had said at the funeral earlier and how he glared at me. Except this time, when I replayed it in my mind, I realized something I hadn't before.

It was possible he wasn't looking at *me* when he said what he had.

It was possible he was looking at someone else.

I thought about those sitting around me, and all at once, everything made perfect sense.

38

I was about five minutes away from Sebastian's house, and neither Foley nor Whitlock were answering my calls. My phone buzzed with a call from a number I didn't recognize. I considered sending it to voicemail to keep the phone line open, but then I answered it.

"I'm … suh, suh sorry."

"Who is this?" I asked.

"I didn't … I didn't mean to do it."

"Sebastian?"

"I meant to … but I didn't mean … I mean …"

He was in hysterics, his voice so unstable, it was hard to make out what he was trying to say.

"I'm almost at your house," I said. "What have you done?"

"I shot him."

"Why?"

"It doesn't matter now. None of it matters now."

I tore down the dirt road, leading to Sean and Meredith's cabin, my headlights beaming into the darkness. Snow was pelting down, the wind whipping in every direction, making it almost impossible to see.

I saw a flicker of something move in front of me, and I put on my high beams. Sebastian was running toward me, gun flailing in his hand. I slammed on the brakes, almost hitting him as the car slid sideways and I skidded to a stop. I reached for my gun and flung my door open, jumping out of the vehicle.

As I walked toward him, I said, "Put the gun down, Sebastian!"

He stared at me, confused, and then he looked down at his trembling hands. A look of shock swept across his face, like he wasn't even aware he was still holding the gun. He looked toward the sky and screamed and then hurled the gun as far as he could throw it.

"You don't understand!" he said. "You don't understand!"

"Then help me understand."

"I had to do it!"

"Where were you going just now?"

"I don't know. Away from here."

"Your father, where is he?" I asked.

"Inside."

"How many times did you shoot him?"

"Once."

"Is he alive?"

"I don't know."

"And your mother? Where is she?"

"My mom was on the phone with the police before I ran out."

"I just want to talk to you, okay?" I said. "You can trust me. It's too cold and too miserable to be out here. Come with me. Let's sit in my car."

Seconds passed.

Sebastian turned away.

I expected him to run, but then he walked to the passenger side of my car and opened the door. I got in and faced him.

"Thank you for trusting me," I said.

"I … I thought you'd want to check on my dad, see if you could save him."

"If your mom called the police, they'll be here soon enough. I want to talk to you before that happens."

He was right to say what he had. Checking on Sean before doing anything else would have been the right thing to do. And maybe I should have felt guilty because I was more concerned about Sebastian's welfare than I was about Sean in that moment. I was starting to understand why Sebastian had shot his father. If I was right, I didn't care much whether Sean lived or died.

"Earlier, at Margot's funeral, I believed you were staring at me when you were talking about avenging Margot's death," I said. "You weren't looking at me, though. You were looking at your father. He murdered Margot, didn't he?"

Sebastian hung his head and nodded.

"When did you figure it out?" I asked.

"The day after Margot went missing, I heard my parents arguing in their bedroom. My mom said something about catching my dad pinning Margot against the wall at our house and trying to kiss her. Guess it happened months ago, right before we broke up."

"Was your dad aware your mother had seen it happen?"

"No, and he tried to deny it, but I've seen him flirt with other women in the past when my mom wasn't around. My mom wouldn't lie, not about that."

"Margot never said anything to you about it?"

He shook his head. "I think it's what she was talking about in the note she left in Bronte's car."

"Let's say you're right, and your father tried to kiss Margot. Kissing her and killing her are two different extremes."

"Why do you think I was sneaking out at night, trying to find out what happened? I went to the trail that night because my dad hikes it twice a week. I thought if he was guilty, he might have taken her there, and I wanted to prove either he did do it or didn't do it."

"And did you?"

"Not at first, and then I noticed my grandfather's old pickup was missing from the garage. I asked my dad where it was, and he said he sold it, but he wouldn't give me any details."

"What color was the pickup?"

"White."

White—just like the paint chips found on Margot's bike.

"I'm guessing you didn't find the pickup?" I asked.

"I didn't. But remember that blue piece of fabric we found? My dad has a blue jacket. He wears it every day in winter, except he hasn't worn it in over a week."

I now understood why Sebastian had been a wreck and had distanced himself from his parents. Not only was he grieving, he was coming to terms with the fact that his own father may have killed the woman he loved.

"Did you look for the jacket?" I asked.

"I've searched everywhere. I haven't been able to find it. I've been keeping things from you, but I didn't want to say anything until I knew for sure."

"And now you know for sure? What is it, Sebastian?"

He rubbed his hands together, took a few deep breaths in, and said, "After the funeral, we all came home, and my dad started humming the beginning of a song. It was one of Margot's favorite songs. She played it a lot when we hung out in my room. I asked him why he was humming that song, and it was as if he hadn't realized he was doing it until I questioned him. He had this look in his eye, and I knew he was guilty."

"What did you do?"

"I went to his gun cabinet and then I went to the den and pointed it at him. I told him if he didn't confess right then and there, I'd shoot him. He blew me off, said I was acting out of anger because I needed someone to blame."

He paused, taking in a few deep breaths, and I urged him to continue.

"I mentioned Grandpa's pickup, the coat, the song," he said. "My mom was standing there, and she looked at me. I thought she was going to defend him at first, but then I think she realized how much sense it made. I kept pushing him to confess, and he kept denying it. He came at me, trying to get the gun away from me, and I shot him. And I ... I stood over him, and I said if he didn't admit what he'd done, I'd shoot him again. That's when he said he killed her, but that it had all been an accident."

39

Foley and Whitlock arrived at Sean and Meredith's home along with an ambulance and a few police officers. Sean was alive. The bullet had penetrated his rib cage but had caused no major damage. He would live, whether he deserved to or not, and Rae and Bronte would have the closure they deserved.

When the police questioned Sean, he was quick to change his story, saying he'd confessed to Margot's murder out of fear for his own life. For the remainder of the night, I assumed he rested easy, thinking he'd find a way to prove his innocence.

The following morning, a news station televised the description of the pickup Sebastian's grandfather had owned. The manager of a storage unit located about an hour outside of Cambria contacted the police a short time later. He was sure he'd rented a unit to a man several days earlier who'd brought in a vehicle in matching the pickup's description. The truck was now in the possession of the San Luis Obispo Police Department being assessed by Silas and the rest of his forensics team.

While we waited for the results, I paid Sean a visit at the hospital.

He was watching a movie when I walked in, and he wasn't pleased to see me.

"Good thing I wasn't dying last night," he said. "I hear you sat in the car with my son until the police arrived instead of doing what you should have done, which was to check on me."

"If you ask me, I made the right call. I'll be honest with you, I hoped you'd die. You deserve to after what you did."

"Whatever my son told you, it's all a lie."

"I hear your father's pickup truck has been located," I said. "The one you were driving the night you hit Margot."

He laughed it off like it meant nothing. "Doesn't mean anything. Lots of people own white pickups."

I crossed one leg over the other. "I just had a long talk with your wife. She told me all about the day you tried to kiss Margot and how Margot had to fight you off. Did you know your wife was planning on divorcing you once Sebastian graduated from high school? That's why she talked you into selling the property."

"I don't know what my wife *thinks* she saw happen, but if she is about to divorce me, it explains why she'd make up such a ridiculous story."

"Do you want to know a story that's not ridiculous? Blood and skin cells were found beneath Margot's fingernails."

"So what?"

"Each person's DNA is unique to them, unless you're an identical twin, which you are not."

"I assume you're telling me this for a reason. Get to the point, and then I want you to get out of here."

"The point is … the coroner believes Margot scratched the person who attacked her before she died. When the doctor was treating your wound last night, he found scratch marks on both of your hips, scratches that drew blood, thanks to Margot's sharp fingernails. You can sit here and deny what you did all you want. We both know you're guilty."

40

Three weeks later

I was sitting in Foley's office, talking to him about Margot's case. "Sean confessed to everything," Foley said. "Didn't have much of a choice, of course. The skin cells under Margot's nails were a match. The blood sample we took from Sean was also a match."

"Did Sean tell you what happened and why he did it?" I asked.

"According to him, Margot went to see Sean at the cabin the morning of the day she disappeared. Sebastian was at work at the time, and Sean was home alone. Margot told him she was meeting Sebastian that night to tell him about the kiss unless Sean came clean and did it before then. Sean drove to Sebastian's work later that afternoon, planning to come up with some story to make Margot look like a liar, no doubt. But when he got there, he chickened out, and he left."

"It's possible he chickened out because it wasn't the first time Sebastian had seen his father being inappropriate with women. He must have been on his way home, and he saw Margot."

"Yep. He claims he was angry, and he hit her without thinking about it. Then he didn't know what to do. My thinking is that he thought he'd kill her if he hit her hard enough, and he could have told everyone she'd darted into the road or some cockamamie story … that it was an accident."

"But he didn't kill her, so he needed a new plan."

Foley nodded. "He scooped her up and put her in the truck before anyone saw what he'd done. He drove out by the trail where we found her, and at some point, she opened the door and jumped out. He took off after her."

"I don't even want to know what happened next, but tell me anyway."

Foley leaned back in his chair, running a hand over his bald head. "It upsets me so much. I don't even like thinking about it. Sean chased after her, and she tripped, hitting her head on a rock. She went down. He said she was still alive, and she tried to fend him off. That's when he, you know, he forced himself on—"

"It's all right. I know what he did next. How did she die?"

"After he violated her, he said she went unconscious and stopped moving. He said she died from the fall she'd had. I don't believe a word of it. I think he cracked her in the head with a rock and killed her."

"And he decided to bury her, right then and there."

"Sean said he panicked. Then he remembered his father always carried a small shovel in the toolbox in the back of his pickup, so he dug a hole and buried her."

"Why lay out her clothing the way he did?"

"He told me everything happened so fast, he didn't have time to think. When he realized what he'd done, he felt awful."

"Sure he did."

"Look, I'm just telling you what he told me."

"Go on," I said.

"He said he'd sat for a while after she died, staring at her, and thinking about his son. That's when he decided to place her in the grave the way he did. I think he did it to make himself feel better about what he'd done."

I sat in silence for a time, my emotions so full, I found myself struggling to speak.

Foley leaned toward me and said, "You okay?"

"No, I'm not. But I'm glad it's all over and that Sean will never be able to hurt anyone again."

I glanced at the time and realized if I didn't leave now, I'd be late for my coffee date with Rae. I left the police department, and on the way over to meet her, I thought about what Margot had said to her friends about Coach Warren. It made sense to me now as to why she thought his actions toward her were a bit inappropriate. After what happened with Sean, I imagine her sensitivity level was heightened. I now believed Warren's story about his actions being unintentional.

Rae was sitting at a table for two, waiting for me when I arrived.

"I ordered for you, if that's okay," she said. "Mocha, skim milk, no whipped cream, right?"

I nodded. "Thank you. How are you doing?"

"I'm a mess, if I'm being honest. But my daughter's killer has been caught, and she's been put to rest in a place where she can be at peace. That means everything to me."

"It will be some time before you start to feel like yourself again. But it will get better, and I will be here every step of the way."

Rae reached out, clasping my hands in hers. "Thank you, Georgiana, for everything. I don't know what I would have done without you."

"You're an amazing woman, Rae. I know you'll get through it. How's Bronte doing?"

"These last few weeks have been hard on her."

"Has she reconciled with Sebastian?"

Rae shook her head. "She still thinks he should have told her he suspected his father from the start. She's still angry, but she'll come around. I've been thinking about him a lot. I can't imagine how he's feeling."

"I saw him yesterday, and he's doing all right. I talked Meredith into hiring a lawyer friend of mine, Tiffany Wheeler, to represent him."

"Do you think he'll serve any time?"

"I hope not. Meredith told the police that Sean lunged at Sebastian, which scared him, and that's why the gun went off."

Rae raised a brow and said, "Do you think her version of events is true?"

"It's similar to Sebastian's version of events. I want to believe it. I understand why he did what he did." I took a sip of my mocha and said, "Have you had any contact with Grant?"

"We've talked on the phone a couple of times, and I'm glad. He's not the one for me, but I don't regret our relationship."

Rae's cell phone rang. She excused herself to answer it, and when she returned, she said, "I hate to get together and run, but it seems I have an emergency. There's a patient I need to see in twenty minutes. Everything's fine, just a sprain."

We hugged, and she waved at me as she made her way out of the diner. I finished my mocha, and as I was leaving, I spotted Isaac sitting across from a young woman.

I approached their booth, and he looked up, nervous to find me standing there.

"Hello, Isaac," I said. "It's been a while."

"Uhh, yeah, hi," he said.

I turned toward the young woman and smiled. "And you are?"

"Hannah."

"Hi, Hannah, I'm Detective Georgiana Germaine. How do you know Isaac?"

"We met last weekend," Hannah said. "This is our first date."

Their first date.

The timing couldn't have been any more perfect.

I turned toward Isaac and said, "Scoot on over. I'll just be a minute, and then you two can get back to whatever riveting conversation you were having."

He looked at me, dumbfounded, and didn't move, so I slid in next to him, using my hip to push him over just far enough to get one of my butt cheeks on the seat.

"Hannah, do you like stories?" I asked.

She shrugged. "Yeah, I guess. Why?"

"Well, you're in luck. There are a few things you should know about this young man here before you make the wise decision *not* to see him again. Where to begin? Let's see now … Four months ago, there was a party, and at this party …"

THE END

Thank you for reading Little Buried Secrets, book eight in the *USA Today* bestselling Georgiana Germaine mystery series.

I hope you enjoyed getting to know the characters in this story as much as I have enjoyed writing them for you. This is a continuing series with more books coming before and after the one you just read. You can find the series order (as of the date of this printing) in the "Books by Cheryl Bradshaw" section below.

In Little Stolen Memories, book nine in the series:

In a secluded cabin deep within the woods, an ominous stranger is about to change the lives of six unsuspecting teenagers forever ...

When Owen ventures outside and mysteriously vanishes, Jackson and Aiden set out to find him. As night descends and the teen boys fail to return, Cora joins in the search. The silence of the woods is shattered when Cora stumbles upon a horrifying discovery—Jackson lying motionless in a pool of his own blood, his fragile life slipping away.

With every moment counting, Cora rushes for help, unaware of the danger lurking nearby. Someone steps out of the shadows, striking her on the side of the head with a heavy object. As her legs buckle beneath her, she sags to the ground, and everything around her goes black.

Little Stolen Memories is a haunting, pulse-pounding mystery of survival, deception, and intrigue that will hold you captive from the heart-stopping beginning to the unimaginable end.

What Readers are Saying about the Series:

"Makes you want to keep reading the story into the night."

"A strong lead character and plenty of drama, it keeps the reader engaged."

"Leaving you wanting to read more."

"You feel like you live close by and can see these characters walking by and waving to you."

"I will definitely read more from this author."

"Kept me on the edge of my seat."

Want a sneak peek? Here's an exclusive look at chapter one …

LITTLE STOLEN MEMORIES

1

Cora Callahan kicked back in the worn leather recliner, smiling as she watched her friends dance to Usher's *Yeah!* in the living room. The plan to take a trip with Brynn and Aubree before the trio headed off to separate colleges in the fall had taken weeks to put in motion. Once the arrangements were made, Cora moved on to step two: convincing her mother to allow her to take a weekend trip without parental supervision. It took some finagling, but in the end, she'd done it.

Her parents believed the three of them were spending the weekend at the beach.

In truth, they were nowhere near it.

They were in the woods at Cora's grandmother's summer cabin.

And they weren't alone … their fellow classmates Aidan, Jackson, and Owen had joined them.

It was the perfect getaway for what Cora was sure would be a weekend none of them would forget. Brynn was dating Aidan, and Aubree was dating Jackson. That left Owen, who had been Cora's next-door neighbor since they were seven.

Cora and Owen had shared many memories over the years, and

in recent months, her feelings for him had begun to change. What started out as a childhood friendship had blossomed into something more, and Cora found herself struggling to decide the best way to tell him. She was ninety percent sure Owen shared her feelings. But that stubborn ten percent kept her lips sealed, and she'd pushed her feelings down, down, down until she'd all but convinced herself she no longer had them.

Tonight, it was all about to change.

Tonight, she'd tell him everything.

Thinking about it now, her heart raced.

"Come on, Cora," Aubree said, waving her over. "Dance with us."

Cora looked at Aubree, whose long, blond hair was bouncing up and down to the beat of the song, and said, "I'm waiting for Owen."

"You don't need Owen in order to dance," Aubree said.

"I know. It's just … we're supposed to go for a walk."

Aubree glanced outside. "In the dark?"

"We have flashlights. We'll be fine."

"Where is Owen, anyway?" Aubree asked. "I haven't seen him for a while."

"He was outside earlier," Jackson said. "He needed to get something out of his car."

"When?" Cora asked.

Jackson shrugged. "I dunno. Been a while, I guess."

Cora shot out of the recliner and walked to the door, opening it, and flicking the porch light on. She cupped a hand to the side of her mouth and shouted, "Owen? Are you out here?"

She was met with silence.

Poking her head outside, Cora glanced in all directions, shouting his name a few more times. She got the same results as before. She pulled a mini flashlight out of her pocket and clicked it on, shining it in the direction of Owen's car.

Nothing suspicious there.

Still, she was beginning to worry.

She stepped back inside the cabin and said, "If he was out here, he isn't now."

"What did you say?" Aubree asked.

Cora walked over to the stereo and lowered the volume. "Owen's not outside. At least he's not answering when I call his name."

"Have you tried looking upstairs?" Jackson asked. "Maybe he's in his room. Brynn and Aiden are in theirs, spending … ahh, time together."

"You can say they're having sex," Aubree said. "We're high school seniors for heaven's sake."

Cora walked upstairs. Owen's door was closed. She knocked on it, waited a minute, and then opened the door, peering inside. Sitting on top of the bed was a coat and a thick pair of socks. Hiking boots were nearby on the floor. Cora assumed he'd been preparing for the walk they'd planned.

If he wasn't here, and he wasn't outside, where was he?

The door across the hall opened and Brynn stepped out. She smiled at Cora and said, "What's everyone doing?"

"I can't find Owen," Cora said. "When did you last see him?"

Brynn ran a hand through her short, auburn hair. "Ahh … I haven't seen him since we arrived, I guess. It's not a big cabin. He's gotta be around here somewhere."

Cora hoped Brynn was right, and she did another sweep of the cabin, looking in closets this time.

Owen was nowhere to be found.

Cora asked everyone gather in the living room to talk about what to do next, and Jackson suggested the girls remain inside while he and Aiden searched outside.

Twenty minutes turned into forty, and the teen boys still hadn't returned.

"Something's wrong," Cora said. "They should have been back by now. Maybe we should call—"

"If we call our parents, it's all over," Aubree said. "They'll kill us for lying about where we are this weekend. I don't know about you two, but I'm not interested in being grounded all summer."

"I'm scared," Brynn said. "I should call my mom."

Cora considered their situation for a moment and said, "Give me five minutes. If I don't find them, we'll make some calls."

"You're going outside?" Brynn said. "You're crazy. Who knows what's out there?"

"I'm not going to sit here and just hope they come back," Cora said.

"Fine," Aubree said, "I'll go with you."

"No way," Brynn said. "You're not leaving me alone, and I'm not going out there."

"Aubree, you stay with Brynn," Cora said. "Give me fifteen minutes. If I'm not back, call your parents."

Cora grabbed Owen's coat off his bed and fished a bigger flashlight out of the kitchen drawer. On the way out, she remembered her grandmother always kept a pair of night vision binoculars behind her jacket. She located them and stepped outside. The forest was quiet tonight, much more so than she remembered it being in years past. It was almost like it had been suppressed somehow, like all the life within had stilled.

She descended the cabin's steps and started down the dirt road, shouting, "Jackson? Aiden? Can you hear me? Owen? Is anyone there?"

When no response came, she lifted the binoculars from around her neck and scanned her surroundings. She saw nothing unusual at first, and then she noticed a hand reaching up from the forest floor—a hand that appeared to be waving at her.

Cora rushed in its direction and found Jackson, his head bloody, eyes fluttering open and closed.

She knelt beside him, grabbing his hand as she said, "Jackson! What happened?"

"Hit me, and I … I fell. Need … go home. You … out of here."

"I'm going to get help. I'll be right back. I promise."

Cora jumped to a standing position. She started for the cabin, and someone stepped out of the shadows, striking her on the side of the head with a heavy object. As her legs buckled beneath her and she sagged to the ground, she looked up, staring in confusion as her surroundings went black.

I hope you enjoyed the sneak peek!

Reserve your copy today in the Cheryl Bradshaw Store at cherylbradshawstore.com.

Enjoy Little Buried Secrets?

You can show your appreciation by leaving a review on Amazon, Barnes & Noble, Apple Books, Google Play, Kobo, or Goodreads. Reviews are always appreciated!

About Cheryl Bradshaw

Cheryl Bradshaw is a *New York Times* and 11-time *USA Today* bestselling author writing in the genres of mystery, thriller, paranormal suspense, and romantic suspense, among others. Her novel *Stranger in Town* (Sloane Monroe series #4) was a Shamus Award finalist for Best PI Novel of the Year, and her novel *I Have a Secret* (Sloane Monroe series #3) was an eFestival of Words winner for Best Thriller.

Raised in California, most of the year she can be found exploring the tropics in Cairns, Australia, or out traveling the world.

NEVER MISS ONE OF CHERYL'S BOOK'S AGAIN!

Sign up for Cheryl Bradshaw's "Killer Newsletter" today to be the first to know when a new book is released and to enter to win fun bookish swag. You'll also receive some fantastic book freebies just for joining!

Learn more by adding yourself to Cheryl's newsletter list on the home page of her online store at cherylbradshawstore.com. Scroll to the bottom of the home page and fill in your email in the "Sign Up and Save" section.

Books by Cheryl Bradshaw

Sloane Monroe Series

Silent as the Grave (Prequel, Book 0)
When the body of Rebecca Barlow is found floating in the lake, private investigator Sloane Monroe takes on her very first homicide.

Black Diamond Death (Book 1)
Charlotte Halliwell has a secret. But before revealing it to her sister, she's found dead.

Murder in Mind (Book 2)
A woman is found murdered, the serial killer's trademark "S" carved into her wrist.

I Have a Secret (Book 3)
Doug Ward has been running from his past for twenty years. But after his fourth whisky of the night, he doesn't want to keep quiet, not anymore.

Stranger in Town (Book 4)
A frantic mother runs down the aisles, searching for her missing daughter. But little Olivia is already gone.

Bed of Bones (Book 5) (USA Today Bestselling Book)
Sometimes even the deepest, darkest secrets find their way to the surface.

Flirting with Danger (Book 5.5) A Sloane Monroe Short Story
A fancy hotel. A weekend getaway. For Sloane Monroe, rest has finally arrived, until the lights go out, a woman screams, and Sloane's nightmare begins.

Hush Now Baby (Book 6) (USA Today Bestselling Book)
Serena Westwood tiptoes to her baby's crib and looks inside, startled to find her newborn son is gone.

Dead of Night (Book 6.5) A Sloane Monroe Short Story
After her mother-in-law is fatally stabbed, Wren is seen fleeing with the bloody knife. Is Wren the killer, or is a dark, scandalous family secret to blame?

Gone Daddy Gone (Book 7) (USA Today Bestselling Book)
A man lurks behind Shelby in the park. Who is he? And why does he have a gun?

Smoke & Mirrors (Book 8) (USA Today Bestselling Book)
Grace Ashby wakes to the sound of a horrifying scream. She races down the hallway, finding her mother's lifeless body on the floor in a pool of blood. Her mother's boyfriend Hugh is hunched over her, but is Hugh really her mother's killer?

Sloane Monroe Stories: Deadly Sins

Deadly Sins: Sloth (Book 1)
Darryl has been shot, and a mysterious woman is sprawled out on the floor in his hallway. She's dead too. Who is she? And why have they both been murdered?

Deadly Sins: Wrath (Book 2)
Headlights flash through Maddie's car's back windshield, someone following close behind. When her car careens into a nearby tree, the chase comes to an end. But for Maddie, the end is just the beginning.

Deadly Sins: Lust (Book 3)
Marissa Calhoun sits alone on a beach-like swimming hole nestled on Australia's foreshore. Tonight, the lagoon is hers and hers alone. Or is it?

Deadly Sins: Greed (Book 4)
It was just another day for mob boss Giovanni Luciana until he took his car for a drive.

Deadly Sins: Envy (Book 5)
A cryptic message. A missing niece. And only twenty-four hours to pay.

Sloane & Maddie, Peril Awaits
(Co-Authored with Janet Fix)

The Silent Boy (Book 1)
In the hallway of a local tavern, six-year-old Louie Alvarez waits for his mother to take him home. A scream rips through the air, followed by the sound of a gun being fired. Louie freezes, then turns, with a single thought on his mind: RUN.

The Shadow Children (Book 2)
Within the tunnels of the historic port city of Savannah, fourteen-year-old Andi Leland has her mind set on freedom—not just for herself but for all the other teens who have come before her.

The Broken Soul (Book 3)
When the party of a lifetime becomes a party to the death, the lines become blurred. Friends become enemies. Drugs become weapons. And that's just the beginning.

The Widow Maker (Book 4)
A friend murdered. A business in trouble. A marriage struggling to survive. And that's just the beginning.

Georgiana Germaine Series

Little Girl Lost (Book 1)
For the past two years, former detective Georgiana "Gigi" Germaine has been living off the grid, until today, when she hears some disturbing news that shakes her.

Little Lost Secrets (Book 2)
When bones are discovered inside the walls during a home renovation, Georgiana uncovers a secret that's linked to her father's untimely death thirty years earlier.

Little Broken Things (Book 3)
Twenty-year-old Olivia Spencer sits at her desk in her mother's bookshop, dreaming about her upcoming wedding. The store may be closed, but she's not alone, and her dream is about to become her worst nightmare.

Little White Lies (Book 4)
When a serial killer sweeps through the streets of Cambria, California, Georgiana Germaine gets swept up into a tangled web of deception and lies.

Little Tangled Webs (Book 5)
What if you knew the person you loved was murdered, but no one else believed you? Eighteen-year-old Harper Ellis knows she's right, and she's prepared to risk her life to prove it.

Little Shattered Dreams (Book 6)
At fifty-five, Quinn Abernathy has been through her fair share of experiences in life. And tonight, her past is coming back to haunt her.

Little Last Words (Book 7)
After living in a verbally abusive relationship for the past six years, twenty-seven-year-old Penelope Barlow has finally found the courage to leave. But can she escape … with her life?

Little Buried Secrets (Book 8)
In a split-second, a car collides with Margot, and she finds herself hurdling through the air, her bike going one way as she goes the other. Her mind whirls in this moment, as she thinks about her life and just how much she doesn't want to die.

Little Stolen Memories (Book 9)
In a secluded cabin deep within the woods, an ominous stranger is about to change the lives of six unsuspecting teenagers forever.

Addison Lockhart Series

Grayson Manor Haunting (Book 1)
When Addison Lockhart inherits Grayson Manor after her mother's untimely death, she unlocks a secret that's been kept hidden for over fifty years.

Rosecliff Manor Haunting (Book 2)
Addison Lockhart jolts awake. The dream had seemed so real. Eleven-year-old twins Vivian and Grace were so full of life, but they couldn't be. They've been dead for over forty years.

Blackthorn Manor Haunting (Book 3)
Addison Lockhart leans over the manor's window, gasping when she feels a hand on her back. She grabs the windowsill to brace herself, but it's too late--she's already falling.

Belle Manor Haunting (Book 4)
A vehicle barrels through the stop sign, slamming into the car Addison Lockhart is inside before fleeing the scene. Who is the driver of the other car? And what secrets within the walls of Belle Manor will provide the answer?

Crawley Manor Haunting (Book 5)
Something evil is coming. Something dark. Something seeking to destroy everything and everyone in its path. And Addison Lockhart is the only one who can stop it.

Till Death do us Part Novella Series

Whispers of Murder (Book 1)
It was Isabelle Donnelly's wedding day, a moment in time that should have been the happiest in her life...until it ended in murder.

Echoes of Murder (Book 2)
When two women are found dead at the same wedding, medical examiner Reagan Davenport will stop at nothing to discover the identity of the killer.

Stand-Alone Novels

Eye for Revenge (USA Today Bestselling Book)
Quinn Montgomery wakes to find herself in the hospital. Her childhood best friend Evie is dead, and Evie's four-year-old son witnessed it all. Traumatized over what he saw, he hasn't spoken.

The Perfect Lie
When true-crime writer Alexandria Weston is found murdered on the last stop of her book tour, fellow writer Joss Jax steps in to investigate.

Hickory Dickory Dead (USA Today Bestselling Book)
Maisie Fezziwig wakes to a harrowing scream outside. Curious, she walks outside to investigate, and Maisie stumbles on a grisly murder that will change her life forever.

Roadkill (USA Today Bestselling Book)
Suburban housewife Juliette Granger has been living a secret life ... a life that's about to turn deadly for everyone she loves.

Made in United States
North Haven, CT
15 January 2024

47519659R00130